Torn Water

JOHN LYNCH

Torn Water

FOURTH ESTATE • *London*

First published in Great Britain in 2005 by
Fourth Estate
An imprint of HarperCollins*Publishers*
77–85 Fulham Palace Road
London W6 8JB
www.4thestate.co.uk

1

A catalogue record for this book is
available from the British Library

ISBN-13 978-0-00-720268-3
ISBN-10 0-00-720268-7

Typeset in Sabon by Palimpsest Book Production Limited,
Polmont, Stirlingshire

Printed in Great Britain by Clays Ltd, St Ives plc

To Mary

He remembers when he was very young standing by water, his whole being fastened to his reflection, which rose from the depths of the pond to sit shimmering on its dark surface. It seemed as if he was peering into his soul, into the dark matter of its substance, and felt a holy hush seize his heart as if, suddenly, the unseen channels of the world ran through his body.

How he had got there or where the pond was he couldn't remember, but he can vaguely recall a hand on his and being led through high rooms, to a large garden, where bees wove dozy patterns in the air. At the bottom of this garden lay the pond, and he remembers a face bending to meet his and whispering that they would be back in a little while. So he stood where he had been

1

left, his small feet pointing at the stonework of the pond's rim. He remembers a wind brewing in the tops of the trees and tearing at the water for a moment before subsiding, his face then coming into focus like a TV channel being tuned.

He remembers believing he felt his soul flee his body to slip into the other him that now sat on the surface of the water. He felt it rise from the wrappings of his skin like a silhouette or the moving negative of a bird in flight, and squirm through the sharp reflection of his other self, beating a glow of joy on the dark water.

How long he was there he can't recall but those moments where he stood threaded to his other self, confused as to which was which, sit like suspended portraits at the very back of his memory. He often wonders if he has left his soul in the bottom of that pond, and that it has lain in the murky waters for years like a scarred jewel, covered in moss and the sediment of decaying fish.

1. The Quarry

Death was his friend. Mr Death dwelt in the spaces between his thoughts. It held his father in its wide blank palm. He had died when James was only eight, nine years before. One day he was there and the next he wasn't, and in his place stood Death with the endless come-on of its smile. As he had grown up James began to understand that Death was the fall at the end of his dreams. He is small and skinny for his age, like a house plant that has been stowed in the darkness of a kitchen cupboard, its pale stems reaching for light that isn't there. His eyes are blue, like the brilliant stab of a winter's sky, and they drink of the world in long distrustful slurps. His skin is freckled and his nose crooked and long. He finds it hard to sit still, and even harder to listen: since his father died, he has always felt poised on the edge of some great event, some momentous occurrence, and that he must be ready at all times, ready for the truth of it all.

He lives with his mother on a housing estate just outside Newry, surrounded by the border and its many secret crossings and pathways. His mother is small like him. She drinks. He believes it is his fault that she does. He believes that he disappoints her. He is supposed to be at school today, but they can keep it. They can keep the brooding silence of their study periods. They can keep their troops of well-heeled boys. He is different. He has always been different, he is a collector of deaths, and he stores them in the cool harbour behind his eyes, calling on them when his father's absence jags the running of his heart. He performs his deaths for anyone who will watch, or sometimes only for his own pleasure, for the closeness he feels to the lost memory of his father.

He walks down Hill Street past the shopkeepers leaning in their doorways, some tugging on cigarettes, their eyes scouring the streets, giving every face that passes them the once-over. He rounds the corner at the bottom and cuts through the deserted market, the steel frames of the stalls standing eerily on the rough concrete. He crosses Chapel Street scarcely looking at the muddle of bric-à-bric that fronts the second-hand shops. He enters the alleyway connecting Chapel Street to Fair

Street, a short dark cobbled passage damp with lichen and urine. Beer cans stud the ground, some faded pale by the sun; he wrinkles his nose as the smell of old piss hits him. He reaches the roundabout at the bottom of the Dublin road and begins to walk the long, high hill towards the border.

A quarter of a mile from the Customs post a police Land Rover sits in a lay-by; he can glimpse slices of the driver's face through its wire-meshed windows. He wonders what it must be like for the men in the vehicle to live their lives wearing a rhino hide for protection, gated from life.

Two hundred yards from the Customs post he sees the roadside café, a small caravan converted to house two griddles and a host of kettles billowing large pillows of steam. A hatch juts out, creaked back on its hinges, and off into the distance articulated lorries line the road like huge boxed caterpillars.

Drivers stand below the awning above the opened hatch, their breakfast baps and steaming coffee fitted in between bouts of talk. James stands quietly at the back. He often comes here to hover on the outskirts of these men. He envies them their lofty cabs, their autonomy, their careless smiles and the pointed fingers of their speech. He has often dreamed at night of sailing across the tarmac of foreign towns and cities, high above the clamour of normal traffic, his all-seeing headlights blistering the upcoming road.

Two women flit back and forth along the hatch of the caravan, their hands glistening with grease as they stuff gaping bread rolls with sausage and bacon, and thrust them into waiting hands, wiping their fingers hurriedly on their aprons before they claim the money. James edges his way to the hatch and quietly asks for a coffee. The skinnier of the two women, black, heavily dyed hair peeping from beneath the edges of her cap, looks at him for a moment. 'You're a funny-looking lorry driver . . .'

He holds his coins out quickly.

'Shouldn't you be at school?'

'No.' He says it quietly, in a flat tone, trying to keep a lid on the exchange.

'Milk?'

'No . . . thanks.'

'Sugar?'

He nods.

'How many?'

'Two.'

He takes his coffee, guides it down from the hatch, bending his head to meet it, and sips before he begins to move off. A man slaps his mug down and asks for a refill of tea. He looks at James, as if he is sizing up livestock in a pen. 'Whereabouts are you from, son?'

'Carrickburren.'

'Carrickburren no less . . . Do you know a fella by the name of O'Brien lives up that way?'

'No . . . Yes.'

'Keeps the dogs . . . Francie O'Brien. He's some fucking horse. What's the name?'

'Mine?'

'Who the fuck else's? The Pope's? Yes, yours.'

'James . . . James Lavery.'

'Conn Lavery's son?'

'Yeah.'

'He was a good man, your old fella . . . The fucking best . . . A true Irishman lived and died.'

James gives his shoulders a shrug. The larger woman in the hatch hands the lorry driver his refill of tea, and as she does so James sidles off to sit on one of the bollards that dot the road. He watches as the man takes his tea and clears his throat with a large hawked spit; he hears the elastic band slap as it hits the tarmac.

'Good to meet you, son.'

He often gets that. The nodded reverence once men find out who his father was. The grunt of respect.

He spends the afternoon at the disused quarry that lies about a mile from his housing estate, eating his packed lunch only when hunger spikes his stomach. The salmon-paste sandwiches taste damp and slimy, reminding the boy of the lorry driver's spit, arcing heavy and dense, landing with a splat on the black-sponge tarmac. He puts the sandwiches to one side, forcing one last bite down his throat.

He sits cross-legged on a shunt of rock that juts over the deepest part of the pond; birds scythe through the sky. Duckweed covers the surface in mats, interspersed with breaks of water the colour of liquorice. The air seems to hang heavy and doleful over the quarry, dense and thickened like the air in a forgotten room. It reminds him of the silences his mother weaves around the memory of his father. He thinks of the screams she carries in her mouth, cries that rise from her lips like disturbed crows when she drinks.

He can remember his aunt Teezy's arms round him, the smell of soda flour and carbolic soap. He can remember the whispered soothings, her rocking him back and forth on her lap. Beyond in the next room, he remembers seeing his mother's face. Around her people stoop to press her hands; suited men, their cigarettes winking like wizards' eyes in the darkened room, and women standing by her, their faces glowing like lanterns of concern. His mother, a coin head silhouette against the flank of her husband's closed coffin. All this a long time ago when his language rose like bubbles in his throat, and popped formless on the point of his lips.

He remembers the squeal of anguish that came from his mother when two men came to the house that day to pay their respects. They stood before the coffin with a stiff lock to their backs, heads stooped, fists clasped at the base of their spines. He can still see the change in his mother's face as they turned to pay their respects to her. A sound came from her mouth that had raised the hairs on the boy's arms and brought tears to his eyes.

He remembers endless nights in dark rooms, his eyes confused between sleeping and waking. Then there were the times when he woke in the middle of the night and felt the presence of someone nearby. He would lie there and listen to the sobs. He knew it was her, his mother, come to stand by his bed and weep hard tears, gin giving her tongue a loosened power, and a longing for the mouth of the one who was gone.

Then there was the time shortly after, when he had stayed with his aunt Teezy in her small house in the centre of town. He had been told that his mother needed some time, that she hadn't been very well, that she needed to be fixed just like a car when the road had got the better of it. He remembers looking up into Teezy's wide face as she told him, and the false smile of courage that his face suddenly wore.

As the sun begins to fade he leaves the quarry, throwing what's left of his sandwiches into the dark water, watching for a moment as they sit on the mat of duck-weed, then disappear. As he climbs a barbed-wire fence to rejoin the main road leading to his housing estate, he frightens a pair of birds into scrambled flight. He looks at them as they veer skywards, watching them strain upwards. He thinks then of the lorry driver and his hushed respect for his father's memory.

'A true Irishman lived and died.' That was what the lorry driver had said. A true Irishman died only for Ireland, didn't he? Ireland herself would tolerate nothing less.

A Young Patriot's Death for Ireland

I love Ireland. I love her small narrow skies. I love her little shape on the maps. I am about to die for Ireland. I will become immortal. I will live in the songs that old men will sing . . . Women will cry in wonder at my heroism. My mother will carry my picture and show strangers who I was, and she will cry. I will take my gun and kill. I will destroy. My blood will be a river that other patriots bathe in, finding strength in my heroism.

She knows, my mother knows. This is the way it has always been. Ireland needs our blood to breathe, she needs our bodies to hold on to herself. My gun is old but it will do the job. I will take as many of them as I can. I will enjoy their dark-eyed fear as my bullets rip into their cold hearts.

I take my leave. I tell my mother to look for me in

the night sky for tonight a new star will be there. She is crying. I tell her I am taking the dark journey. I tell her I will be joining my father tonight in Ireland's heaven, where the rivers are green like our fields. Yes, I tell her tonight, I will be with my father in Heaven, two true Irishmen lived and died. She smiles, even though she is crying.

The barracks is quiet. I tell the desk sergeant that my mother's car has been stolen. He doesn't glance at me but looks at his watch as I talk. I wait until a couple of his colleagues join him and then I rip my gun from the shopping-bag I'm carrying. I enjoy the surprise that flits across their faces and the lost expressions in their eyes. I kill two of them before I am shot. Not a bad return. As life leaves my ripped body I see heaven hover before me like an vast alien spaceship. Manning its bridge and beckoning me aboard is my father, another true Irishman lived and died.

2. Sully

'Get up . . . James, up.'

'What?'

'Up . . . Out of it and up.'

He opens his eyes. His mother is standing over him, barking at him. She is hung-over: he can tell by the sideways droop of her head.

'Come on . . . Up. We have a visitor.'

'Who?'

'Sully.'

'Shit.'

'Hey . . . None of that . . . Two minutes . . . And up.'

She leaves the bedroom. He catches her taking a peek at herself in the wall mirror as she exits, running a moistened finger across her eyebrows. She has a thing

12

about her eyebrows, always teasing and pulling at them, coaxing them into arced crescents. It revolts him. She revolts him. Sully revolts him.

Sully was his mother's on-off, come and go boyfriend. He arrived one May evening five years before, announced by the rasp of his van's exhaust as it growled along their estate. James had been in the front field, guillotining the tops of ragweed with his hands and feet, when he heard the vroom of Sully's arrival. He had run to the hedge that bordered the estate and arrived just in time to see Sully get out of the van and run the toe of each shiny shoe on the back of his flared trouser legs before he saun-tered up to the front door. James had watched the flush come to his mother's cheek as she had greeted him, the shyness with which she had received the small box of chocolates, then offered her lips to him, closing her eyes in a way that James found devastating.

'Hey, kid – Luke Sullivan. My friends call me Sully, but you can call me Luke.'

He can remember looking up into his cat-grin face, squinting into the blister of the afternoon sun as it peeped out from behind Sully's head. He can remember the nervous way the man had tousled his hair, and how his mother had glared at him from behind Sully's back.

'Get up.'

Eventually, he jumps out of bed and dresses, pulling on his jeans over his pyjama bottoms, cursing softly in the cold air. He can hear their giggles down on the pathway leading up to the front house.

'Come on and see what Sully has brought us.'

Sully was back with his maudlin country music and his taunting smile. Crawling back to terrorise his mother once more, as he always has, as it seems he always will.

'James, come and see,' his mother shouts. She sounds like a fishwife, her voice cutting through the still morning air.

What had he brought this time? What peace-offering was he laying at her feet? Once it had been bricks freshly lifted from a building site he was working on. He had proudly shown them to James, saying that he was going to build his mother 'the finest and securest garden shed known to man'. Another time it was the carcass of a freshly killed pig, which he had hung proudly from a hook in the garage, saying it was a neighbour's and that it had strayed out on to a busy road. He said that it had been looked after like a child when alive and that it would melt in their mouths. His mother screamed when she saw it, throwing her hands to her face and running for the house.

He thuds his way down the stairs and steps out of the front door, working up a large fist of spit in his mouth, hawking it deep from within his throat, then launching it just like the lorry driver had done the week before.

'Look! Look, Jimmy – oh, please, don't do that. You're not an animal.'

No, but Sully is. He looks at them both. They look like they're posing for a photograph. On the pathway lies a huge mound of logs. It reminds him of a large goat dropping. His mother stands beside Sully, as if she has just won a raffle. So that was it, that was his penance: a mound of wet, mouldy logs.

'Hi, kid. Long time no see,' Sully says.

'For fuck's sake.' He says it quietly as he turns to go back in.

'What did you say?' his mother asks.

'What?'

'What did you say?'

'Nothing.'

'Don't be disrespectful.'

'He says it.'

'He's an adult. He can use those words.'

'Leave him be, Ann,' Sully says.

Before Sully there had been other men. James noticed that they all had the same tight force in their eyes. Some stayed longer than others, and some were so brief that their faces melted quickly from memory like a lantern lighting a man's way home slowly being swallowed by blackness.

He can remember looking up into each new face, his eyes narrowed in distress as yet another stranger tried to woo him. Sometimes James believes he dreamed some of them, but he knows this was not the case.

He remembers being in bed one night. He woke and felt the presence of someone sitting at the end of it. He can remember his body freezing in a spasm of fear. The smell of cheap whisky filled the room, and the pale sickly scent of aftershave.

It was a builder his mother had met a few weeks before. A large shaven-headed man, who didn't smile but viewed the world with thin-lipped distrust. When he had been introduced to James he had bent down stiffly extending his hand, his scalp pitted and cracked with scars. His eyes were large and seemed to bore straight into James. He didn't like the man. He didn't like the way he shadowed his mother as if she was a lassoed calf, following her about the house, watching every move she made. His left arm was covered in tattoos, deep blue-green drawings of half-clad women, their cartoon bodies pouting from the bristle of his arm. He frightened James, and when he was in their house there seemed nowhere to escape to, because he seemed to fill every part of it.

They had brought James with them to the local working-man's club earlier that night. He can remember riding in the back seat of the builder's Ford Granada. The seats smelt musty and were covered with dog-hair, and the ashtray in the well between the two seats was full of mint-humbug wrappers. The journey seethed with silence, punctuated only by the squeak of the passenger seat's visor as his mother pulled it down to check her makeup in the mirror.

Excitement scurried in his stomach as he looked forward to his evening at the club. His mother had told him earlier that the only reason they were bringing him was that she couldn't find a babysitter and he was too young to be left on his own.

He can remember the layers of smoke that hung in the air, the cigarette butts and the dried circles of spit dotting the floor like ringworm rounds. It was a large cavernous room with long runs of fluorescent lighting, filled with steel-tube chairs. Groups of drinkers sat together, ringed by empty and half-empty glasses. They were mostly men, their nicotine fingers jabbing the air like small yellow stems.

Young men carried laden trays of drinks to and fro, their slim hips slipping expertly between cluttered tables. They all wore white shirts and flared black trousers, and pocketed their tips quickly with deft thrusts of their hands.

At one point a man stopped by the table. He knew the builder and greeted him with a soft punch on his shoulder. 'Hi, Clive, how's it hanging?' He had only one eye, and the left side of his face was disfigured by a twisted mesh of scars.

Clive greeted the man as 'Nelson', then winked at James's mother and laughed. James couldn't take his eyes off him. He thought Nelson looked like a mannequin after it had been caught in a shop blaze. The man was drunk and at one point threw a look at James, staring at him with his one good eye, his head bobbing to a jaunty tune it seemed that only he could hear. James remembers trying to avoid looking at the scar, the dense shadow that nestled there.

Before he left Nelson turned to Clive and stuck out a hand. After a moment Clive reached into his pocket and placed a few coins in the man's palm. James watched him walk away, and noted that he hadn't said thanks, just took the money and moved on to the next table and hit a small wiry man who sat there a punch of greeting on the shoulder. James had been put at a small side-table, next to his mother's larger one, and given a Lucozade and a bag of crisps. He remembers his feet dangling from his chair, banging against its steel limbs. He watched as Clive and his mother sat and sipped their drinks, staring into the middle distance like people who had just suffered a loss.

As soon as they had finished, one of the young waiters was called over and a new tray of drinks arrived.

Periodically Clive would throw a hopeful glance at James's mother. James remembers how her eyes glittered. She looked as if her mind was hunting, stalking some hidden paradise, far beyond the thin walls of her life.

By the end of the evening they had been joined by a young red-headed man, his skin the colour of milk. He sat beside James's mother and seemed to know her quite well, a little sly smile coming to his face whenever he spoke to her. James can remember watching the three, from his side-table, sipping his flat Lucozade noting how their bodies were halved by the table-top. He became fascinated by the shuffling dance of their legs beneath it, seeing the red-head's feet slide to within inches of his mother's, his right foot begin tickling her ankle knot. Above, in the more visible half, he saw a smile flash across her lips and watched as she dipped her head.

'I love this woman . . .' Clive said suddenly, his body trembling with the force of his declaration. He leant into the middle of the table. He was now inches from the young man's face. 'I fucking love this woman.'

This time it had the force of a confessional whisper, an offered secret, and James watched as, beneath the table, his mother allowed the young red-head's hand to advance slowly along the creamy run of her thigh.

James remembers feeling sorry for Clive. He felt anger towards his mother, a hard violent anger that wanted to stamp on the woman that had risen from the froth of beer and the snatched swallows of gin.

So, later that night, as he slowly opened an eye and peered at Clive sitting at the end of his bed, he felt fear give way to pity. He remembers seeing his bare torso glistening like lard in the moonlight, one hand laid across his belly. He was crying. He seemed to be saying something half to himself, half to the sleeping world. How long he sat there James cannot remember, but eventually his eyes closed, the big man's mutterings lowering him into sleep. He never saw Clive again, and knew better than to enquire as to his whereabouts. Sometimes he thought of him, and saw him lumbering across the landscape of his life, half of it hidden, the other half too painful to behold.

'Glad I'm back, kid. I tell you what, I aim to be here a while this time.'

He is in the kitchen, filling the kettle. Sully has followed him into the house, leaving his stash of freshly thieved logs.

'Listen, kid . . .'

James notices that Sully always addresses him as if they were characters in a Western, opening his shoulders and squinting into the middle distance, especially when he feels unsure. It irritates James: it makes him feel as if Sully isn't really seeing him, that he is just something in the way.

'Those logs will come in handy on the long nights.'

James doesn't reply, pretending not to hear.

Sully sticks his oil-stained hands under the running tap. 'I said –'

'I'm not interested.' James looks deep into his eyes.

Sully just looks back and for a moment they stay that way as if they are lovers about to kiss. Then Sully says, 'Holy cow! If looks could kill, kid, I'd be a dead man.'

Death for the Burning Power of His Mother's Love

They thought I didn't know. They thought I didn't see. They had plans and they didn't include me. After all I had done for her. Everything is clear to me now. She never loved me. She thinks only of herself, like he did. You see, they were one of a kind. As I stand here on the scaffold I think of all the times I have cared for her, looked out for her. I was her guardian. I know it sounds silly, a young son being his parent's guardian, but that's the way it was. That's the way it has always been.

I thought he had gone for good. I thought that we had seen the last of the smug, slap-happy Sully. I was wrong. I knew then something had to be done, that drastic measures were required to stop this man in his tracks. A small crowd has gathered. Some of the men in the crowd shout insults at me. All night long I have waited for this moment, listening from my cell as the workmen put the final touches to the wooden scaffold outside.

I think of the knife I stuck into Sully's heart, the knife that now lies at the bottom of the lake. I think of it buried in the silt. I think of the look of dismay that creased his face as the blade dug deep into his chest. I think of how I had used it to skin him, to gut him, and the hook to hang his carcass from the beam in our outhouse, just like the pig he brought home for her once.

I hear the trapdoor snap open and feel my feet plummet from me and a hard crack travel from the base of my spine as my neck breaks. Through the last thrashing spasms of my body I hear her call my name and see her face lift towards mine, but by then I am far beyond her, swimming in the depths of the lake, pushing down towards my gashed love for her, which lies buried hilt deep in the soft heart of the lake's bed.

3. Teezy

'Don't say anything.'

'I won't.'

'Come on, Jimmy, don't be like that.'

'Like what?'

'You know full well like what. Just don't say anything to her about Sully.'

'All right.'

'I just don't want to get into it with her. Sticking her nose in.'

'All right, Mum. All right.'

They are driving to his aunt Teezy's. A week has passed since Sully's return and his mother has been lost to him. She has run to the sanctuary of Sully's arms and hidden from him there. The pile of logs has stayed where it was dumped, bringing impatient looks from some of the neighbours, and one or two loud grunts of disapproval from Mrs McCracken across the way.

He is fond of Teezy. She is his ally. She is his great-aunt, his grandfather's sister, his father's aunt. His grandfather died before he was born. He had been a brickie, segmenting the world into brick-size pieces, adding mortar and building walls to seal the perimeters of his life. Beyond that James knows nothing, except that Teezy had loved his father dearly, but what is gone is gone.

She is a heavy woman, with soft, large shoulders. Sometimes when she is cooking she rolls up the sleeves of her cardigan, revealing Popeye-like arms and the little gathered parcels of flesh that hang about her elbows.

He feels safe with her, with the bulky force of her ways. She always keeps a bottle of Bols Advocaat on a high shelf in her living room, and at the end of the day she ceremoniously pours a capful into a waiting thimble glass. Then she sits by her small television set, prises her shoes from her feet and gently caresses the small bones of her ankle with one of her toes.

James had noticed from a very early age that there are two Teezys. First there is the serene Teezy, the 'end-of-day woman', with her glass, holding the world outside at arm's length. On the other hand there is the 'street' Teezy, who barges her way across town. A woman who

is larger and angrier, who forces her way through check-
points and grumpily ignores bomb scares, shouting at
the top of her voice that it is her country and that no
one is going to stop her buying her eggs.

'My goodness, you are shooting up. You're still a bit
mealy-looking, mind. A good feed would do you the
world of good – do you hear me, Ann?'

'You saying I don't feed my son, Teezy?'

They have arrived. Teezy is ushering them through the
narrow corridor of her small townhouse, clucking and
fussing like a mothering hen.

'No, not at all, but sometimes, you know as well as
I do, you have to stand over them.'

'Well, I've better things to do, Teezy, no harm to you.'

'Yes, and it begins with an S.'

She says it quietly, out of his mother's earshot; it brings
a smirk to James's lips.

'What did he bring this time?' she whispers to him.

'A pile of logs.'

'The romantic.'

One year he got hives. He remembers clawing at them
with his fingernails, trying to avoid the heads, drawing
red tracks either side of them, itching so much and so
often that he numbed his arm. He remembers Teezy
slopping palmfuls of calamine lotion all over his body,
rebuking his cries by declaring firmly,

'Too many scallions.

'Not enough sleep.

'Too many tomatoes.

'Not enough greens.'

Almost immediately the calamine lotion would dry into a crust, the heads of the hives peeping through in weeping clusters.

Teezy and his mother had got together for the evening about a year after his father had died and they were preparing James for bed, fussing around him. His mother was drawing a large hairbrush across his head in hard arcs, bringing tears to his eyes. 'You've hair like strips of wire,' she had said, grunting as she pulled the brush across his skull. 'Stubborn, stubborn hair.'

'I wonder where he got that from,' Teezy had said.

As the evening had worn on the two women had filled the house with their laughter. Every now and again James's mother would turn to him, eyes misty with booze, and ask him thickly if he was all right, if his hives itched, and if they did not to touch them. He remembers feeling like a prisoner held captive in his own body, encased in the chalky suit of dried lotion.

At one point Teezy had insisted that she was not able for more drink, raising her hand like a policeman stopping traffic.

'What sort of a woman are you?' his mother had said.

'Oh, all right then, a wee one.'

James can remember seeing Teezy's glass welcome the

sherry. It was the first and only time that he had seen his auntie drunk, the only time he had seen her take on his mother at her own game. Slowly the two Teezys blurred into one, and the angrier, the 'street' one, began to hold sway. Once she looked over at James in a way that prompted the hairs on the back of his neck to stand up, and caused his skin to itch once more.

His mother, he remembers, never took her eyes off Teezy. At the moment Teezy had looked at James, his mother had placed a record on the old deck she kept beneath some magazines by the television set. Then she began to yelp and dance at the edge of Teezy's vision, thumping her feet down heavily on the linoleum, and slowly began to advance on her.

It took a moment for Teezy to release James from her gaze and turn to look at Ann, a smile breaking across her face. She then had leapt to her feet, clapping her hands.

The two women began to dance. He watched as they made little jinking runs around one another, their arms held out from their bodies. When a slower ballad came on they looked at each other and laughed, and Teezy eased her body back into the fireside chair. His mother had then turned to James and offered him her outstretched arms, her eyes gaily dancing like the flames in the dark mouth of the grate. 'Come on, dance with me,' she had said. 'Dance with your queen.'

* * *

'Right, I'm off,' His mother says.

They stand in Teezy's small scullery as if at a wake, unsure what to say or do.

'You've things to do yourself, haven't you, Jimmy?'

'Yeah.'

'See you in a bit, then.'

'Send my regards to the reprobate,' Teezy says.

'Did you tell her?' his mum asks him.

'No.'

'I may be old but I'm not stupid, Ann,' Teezy shouts after her.

He can remember the way her skin had slipped on to his like moss along a stone. He can remember her breath on his neck, the way she told him to put his sockless feet on her shoes. He remembers climbing on to them, and feeling his soles lie across the bridge of her feet. He remembers them moving together.

'My strong man . . . my fierce, strong little man,' she had said.

The song had finished and his mother asked quietly how his hives were; all right, he had said. They were still close together, his mother leaning down to meet the smile in his eyes.

'If Conn was only here to see you . . .' his auntie had suddenly said, her head nodding, the fire beating a crimson glow on the side of her face.

Suddenly his mother's eyes had clouded. She turned and ripped the LP from the turntable. A silence sat, fat and solid, in the air. He remembers inching his way back to his seat, its springs squealing as he sat.

James remembers turning the name quietly on his tongue, like a small fiery sweet, Conn . . . his father's name. A four-lettered bomb exploding in his heart. Conn . . . Conn . . . like a fist in his mind, Conn . . . Conn . . . Conn.

'Don't ever mention his name again,' his mother had said.

And with that she had retaken her seat, and filled her near-empty glass, the liquid spilling across its lip. The two women had sat in angry silence until his mother lifted the glass to her mouth.

He can remember sitting there, his small fists clenched, dried peels of calamine lotion falling on to the crotch of his pyjama bottoms, watching the two women glare at one another. He began to itch and scratch at his hives.

'Don't,' his mother had said.

He had stopped and held out his hands towards her, palm upwards, in protest, in defiance, sitting there, knowing that if a secret wore skin it would look something like his.

'Do you not eat, son?'

'Yeah . . . No . . . I'm fine, Teezy.'

'You look like a pale streak of nothing. No harm to you . . .'

He sits alone with Teezy in her scullery. He can imagine his mother scurrying down the town, bustling past shoppers, on her way to meet the heathen Sully.

Teezy stands and gives him a twinkly smile. He turns her head away from her. He knows that look: he knows what's coming.

'What about you, my boy?'

'What about me?'

'Are there any little ladies in your life that I should know about?'

'No.'

That sounds a bit final, son.'

'Teezy, please.'

'Come on, son.'

'What?'

'You're so serious, son. Have a bit of fun. Find a nice young strip of a thing and have a bit of a time with her.'

'Yuk.'

'Yuk? What sort of a word is that? Your schooling needs to be shaped up, my boy. Yuk . . . Come on, son, lighten up those chops of yours.' She leans down to him, her eyes full of mischief.

'Teezy . . .'

'You've a face on you would freeze milk and hell besides. Come on, let me fix you something and we'll have a chuckle together.'

'I'm fine, Teezy.'

'You're going to waste away, son, with that serious mug of yours, disappear before our very eyes.'

'I think he's back to stay for good this time, Teezy.'

'I know, son, I know . . . How about a nice boiled egg?'

Death from an Acute and Unrelenting Hunger

The fields are blackened from the blight. I can see some of my neighbours crawling across the soil scrabbling for one healthy potato. I feel sorry for them. I cannot remember the last time I ate, for in my dreams I have always been hungry. My mother died a few days ago, followed quickly by my aunt Teezy. They died in each other's arms. I didn't have the strength to bury them, and had to leave them where they fell.

Once I believed that God had given me the power to save everyone by teaching them how to eat stones and the fine dust that fell from the cracks of buildings, but no one would listen. Another time I believed that the clouds were edible and spent days building a flying machine from twigs and the trunk of a fallen tree, but I must have misheard God's instructions for it refused to fly.

Most of the time, though, I just sit on the headland that fronts my small village, watching the sea. Sometimes

I think I can see my mother dancing in the waves.

It is late now and God is talking to me again. I like it when God speaks to me, I like the way it soothes my heart, and the way the world expands like a mouth being kissed.

I stand. My slender body sways like a leaf on a branch. I smile to myself as I realise suddenly that God has given me wings and that I am climbing to the roof of the world to join my mother, and that my hands are full of clouds and the icy sparks of stars. My flight doesn't last and before long the cold night sea is travelling towards me at speed. By then, though, it is too late to change my mind.

4. Outer Space

When he was younger he was obsessed with the pictures of the Apollo astronauts. He remembers the lonely slope of their shadows on the moon's lifeless surface and the blackness surrounding them, as if on every hand there was mystery. He remembers wondering if that was where his father had gone when he died – is that where everyone went? Did they melt into the darkness that held the earth and the other planets captive?

Sometimes he thought he could hear his father's cries for help, and he pictured him spiralling like a satellite in the outreaches of space, his body slowly blackening. He would wake and rush to his bedroom window, his eyes scouring the night sky, his heart yearning to join his father in the depths of the universe.

He had tried to tell his mother that he believed his father was lost far, far out in the cosmos. He had tried to tell her one morning, years before, as she had faced him across the breakfast table. He remembers the frustration of not being able to say the words, to push them from his lips. He remembers his mother scowling with impatience, sharply telling him to eat his breakfast and to stop the nonsense. Eventually he had stood, limbs quivering with frustration. Then he had yelled it, as if his life depended on it: 'Daddy is with the astronauts! I heard him! I heard him crying . . .'

His mother had slowly placed her fork on the plate and stood, carefully pulling the creases free in her skirt. Then she had walked to where he was standing. She had clamped her hands beneath his armpits and lifted him up, then slammed him back into his seat. He had landed with a jolting shudder that banged his jaw shut. She had leaned very close into his face, and had wordlessly cautioned him, her eyes unblinkingly facing his.

It is the end of the second week of Sully's return. They are on Sully time: everything his mother says and does revolves around him. She is standing by the kitchen door. Her hair is mussed; a piece of toast hangs from her lips. Sully has just left, having stayed the night. He's only back and already they're playing Happy Families.

'Sully wants to take you see Northern Ireland play.'

'I don't like Northern Ireland,' James says.

'What's that supposed to mean? You're Irish, aren't you?'

'That's what I mean.'

'Oh, don't start that. Football's just football.'

'No, it's not.'

'He's making a real effort this time, Jimmy. Come on, meet him half-way.'

'Why are you back with him?'

'That's between him and me.'

'No, it's not. I live here too . . . or had you forgotten?'

'Don't be cheeky or –'

'Or what, Mum? Or what? You'll get Sully for me?'

'Jesus.'

He slams the door on his way out and glares at Mrs McCracken as she stands in her doorway opposite theirs, her eyes lifting disapprovingly from the untouched pile of logs to meet his. 'Is someone going to do something about those logs?'

But he ignores her and begins to walk towards the town.

'Here, son, this is for you . . .'

He can remember looking up into Teezy's eyes as he took the photograph from her. He can remember the look on her face as if it was about to break.

'That's your daddy.'

It was a small, dog-eared photograph of a man

standing against a hill, squinting into the sunlight, right hand raised playfully to his face.

'He died for Ireland . . . Sssh,' she had said, as if the world was listening.

'Sssh,' he had replied, cooing it up into her face. 'Sssh.'

'Now, no more astronauts, no more stories. They only upset your mammy.'

'Sssh.'

For days afterwards he had wandered around, whispering it within earshot of the grown-ups. 'Sssh,' he remembers saying, putting his small face close to his mother's. 'Sssh.'

'It's our secret. It's our private story,' Teezy had said, as she had given him the photo. 'Wasn't he a fine-looking man? As fine as Ireland herself.'

'Sssh,' he had said.

'This is your father . . . He died for Ireland.'

He remembers how he had looked at the worn photograph, at the slender figure that grinned at him through the fallen years. Sometimes now he would bring it out from its hiding-place and quietly gaze at it, his eyes hunting its held landscape. He would hold the photo delicately as if it was made of silk. At other times he would quietly curse the man, damn him for leaving, hate him for his absence, his fingernails digging into the photo's edge so that they left crescent-shaped marks.

* * *

'Watch where you're going, sunshine.'

'Sorry.' He looks up into the fuck-you face of Malachy O'Hare, the estate hard man.

'IRA or Prod?'

'What?'

'IRA or Prod?'

James looks across at Malachy's troops, small, hard-faced boys. 'For fuck's sake, IRA.'

'Don't curse when you say it. Don't disrespect the flag.'

'Sorry . . . IRA.' He goes to slide past them, careful not to look any of them directly in the eye.

'Hold on a minute, sunshine. Do us one of your deaths.'

'What?'

'Jimmy Lavery, the Death Machine. Do us one of your deaths.'

'Give us a break.'

'Do one . . . or else.' He raises a large fist to the tip of James's nose.

'OK.'

'Good man yourself.' Malachy's face breaks into a big, muggy smile. 'What have you got for us today?'

James looks skywards, and after a moment he says, 'Well, there's this astronaut . . . and he's lost his mother ship . . .'

'An Irish astronaut?' Malachy asks.

'Yeah, an Irish astronaut.'

An Astronaut's Final Message

Time: 0900 hours
Location: Support Capsule
      The Erin Galaxy
Date: 12 Dec 2157
Message Received From: Captain Conn Lavery.
Dear Ann and Little Jimmy,
By the time you receive this transmission I will be
dead. As I write this I am slowly suffocating. For
the last hour I have been using my spacesuit's
reserve tank of oxygen, but even that now has
begun to fail. The mother ship is ablaze, I can see it
beyond, through my small porthole window, and it
looks like a devil's eye, hot and fiery. All my
comrades are aboard her, good strong men, with
only one love in their lives: Ireland. It is strange to
think that I will never see either of you again, that I
will never hold you close and feel the full warmth
of your bodies.

I hope you both remember me fondly, as a true
Irish spaceman. We fought hard, my son, harder
than you can ever know. We repelled the alien
hordes three times before their greater military

strength began to tell. We all die, son, we all die, and we must be grateful for the time we have had together. It is strange to think that space will be my grave; the huge black belly of space will be a mausoleum for my bones. Look after your mammy, my son. Let no one come between her and my memory. I love you both dearly, more than you can know. I have decided to leave my capsule, the oxygen has gone, and the little I have left in my spacesuit I'm hoping will sustain me on my walk to meet the face of God. I'm stepping clear of the capsule now . . . Air is going quicker than I thought. I love you both. Look for a new star tonight in the sky.

Love for as long as there is any, Captain Conn Lavery.
End Of Transmission.

5. *The Rehearsal*

He is following Mr Shannon, scrambling behind him, trying to keep up with his long strides, down High Street and across the Mall. The streets are full of schoolchildren scurrying for buses and with shoppers flitting in and out of stores.

'Keep up, Lavery, keep up. You're letting the side down, old boy.'

Shannon seems to glide along on his own current of air, swaying to avoid a pack of schoolgirls, tipping his head in greeting to people he knows. James collides with a small dog, its body contracting into yelps as his foot finds its paw. Shannon comes to a halt and looks back at the dog, hopping around on three legs, and at James scurrying after it.

'Hit it a boot in the hoop, Lavery, and look lively. *Tempus fugit*. Good day, Mrs O'Rourke.'

Mrs O'Rourke stares at James and pushes him away as he tries to make amends with her dog. 'Clear off, you hooligan.'

'I'm sorry,' he whimpers.

'Piss off before I take a lump out of you. Good afternoon, Mr Shannon, you're looking well this fine day.'

'One can but try, Mrs O'Rourke, one can but try.'

He watches as Shannon struts away from him, delicately sidestepping a pushchair, full of fruit and groceries.

Mr A. G. S. Shannon is James's English teacher, 'a force for literature', as he likes to call himself. James can remember the first time Shannon had stood before him in classroom G14, seven years before, giving his new English lit charges the once-over. He wore moccasins and James can remember their slap on the floor as he paced, his heels making a small sucking noise as his feet travelled back and forth. His hair in those days was a Brylcreemed black with a kiss-curl that fell daintily across his wide forehead. It was his belly, though, that fascinated James: it was large; it seemed to begin at his sternum and end at his groin. James thought it looked as if it had been grafted on to his body for it seemed at odds with the relatively slender man that carried it.

'My name is Mr A. G. S. Shannon and my business is literature, and your business is to make it your business.' Then he had lifted his head and raised an index finger to his chin. 'If you have knowledge of language, my boys, you have a shot at the truth. Without it you will remain in your Neanderthal twilight, grunting and pawing your way through life.'

Some boys had burst out laughing, some had let out a snort of protest, but James and a couple of others had held the thought he had given them as if it were fashioned from gold. He was different from the rest of the teachers. He didn't seem to have the same cranky dedication to authority, or the constant need to flex it. James would often hang around at the end of class, waiting to catch his eye, to be fed a small morsel of his attention. Sometimes he would put his arm across James's shoulders and walk him from the class. They would amble down the corridor, Mr Shannon's rich quotes from Shakespeare weaving seamlessly with the strong blades of sunlight streaming through the windows.

Rehearsals are in an old two-storeyed townhouse off Canal Street. The front door lies open, revealing a long, narrow hall lit only by a solitary lightbulb, with a wooden staircase at the end. They climb to the top floor, Shannon sometimes taking two, three steps at a time. Two men he has never seen before stand by a fireplace. Shannon guides him towards them, his hand delicately placed between the boy's shoulder-blades. The men look up from two tattered scripts; one wears a Paisley cravat.

'Gentlemen, may I introduce you to young James Lavery? He is our Martini. Lavery, this is Cathal Murphy.'

The man wearing the Paisley cravat extends his hand, and James shakes it shyly.

'And this reprobate, Lavery, is the inestimable Oisin "Chin Chin" Daly.'

Oisin "Chin Chin" Daly is at least six feet tall, with long, greasy, heavy hair. He has brown eyes that flicker watchfully from behind a pair of wire-rimmed glasses. 'Mr Lavery . . .'

'Mr Chin Chin – sorry, Oisin.'

'No, man, you scored the first time.'

Suddenly two women are in the doorway. One is small with red, short-cropped hair and a freckled face; on her shoulder is a green duffel bag with white trim. The other rummages furiously in one of two plastic shopping-bags. She is plump and short with greying brown hair.

Shannon eyes her imperiously, left eyebrow arched. 'Ah, Nurse Ratshit at long last.'

'Ratchet, Nurse Ratchet, you bollocks. Where the f— ing hell are my car keys?' Suddenly she notices a set hanging from her friend's hand. 'For Chrissakes, Patricia, why didn't you pipe up? And me making a complete arse of myself.'

'You gave them to me not two minutes ago, Kerry, in case you lost them.'

The play they are there to rehearse is *One Flew Over*

the Cuckoo's Nest. James has been roped in to play Mr
Martini, a paranoid character who spends most of the play
talking with an imaginary friend. Mr Shannon had crept
into the physics class the week before and asked permission from Mr Bennett to steal James for ten minutes.

'Of course, Mr Shannon, have him for as long as you'd
like.'

As they stood in the science corridor, Shannon had
dug a thin book out of his briefcase, and held it skyward,
an awkward grin of triumph spreading across his lips.
'Do you know what this is, Lavery? Do you have any
idea?'

'No, sir.'

'An American classic, Lavery, a modern classic from
the New World.'

'Yes, sir.'

'I want you to peruse it.'

'Sir?'

'Read it.'

'Why, sir?'

'Because you are going to be in it.'

'Me?'

'Yes. Your part is Martini. Rehearsals begin next
Tuesday afternoon after school. Performance in the
amateur drama festival at the Opera House, Belfast, one
month from now.'

'Why me, sir?'

'Why not you, Lavery? Pray, why not you?'

James had watched as Shannon walked away from him, backside swaying, head held high. Just before he turned the corner he raised the fingers of his right hand and wiggled them.

Back in the physics class, he had turned the booklet over and over in his hands.

'What's that?' Seamus Byrne, the boy next to him, had asked, when Bennett wasn't looking.

'A play.'

'A what?'

'A play.'

'You poof.'

A week later, against his better judgement, there he is. With everyone now seated and settled, Mr Shannon calls for order, his briefcase resting on his knees. A curt businesslike smile announces that their evening's work is at hand. Behind them is the fireplace, full of debris, half-burnt parish circulars and cigarette packets. Barely at first, James sees the shape of something else lurking in it, blacker than shadow, a dead crow, its head wrenched and twisted back on itself, its beak frosted with ash.

'Now, business of the first order . . . We have a new addition to our ranks, Master Lavery from Carrickburren. Lavery will be playing Martini.'

All faces are smiling at him. Cathal Murphy gives him a playful dig in the ribs, the two women whisper to each other and one blows him a kiss. Most excruciating of all, he can feel the doting beam of Mr Shannon's stare.

'As you can probably surmise, we are a little short-staffed at the moment, due to teaching commitments, babysitter shortages . . . and downright laziness. But do not despair, all will be well – once I've broken a few heads.'

A siren wails outside. Shannon tries to speak but swallows his sentence, letting the noise bleed through and out of range. 'Well, after that rather apt fanfare, let us get down to business. Mr Lavery, let us take a bold step. I would like us to begin this evening with the nightmare sequence involving your character, Mr Martini, and his brutal, painful memories of a particular airborne dogfight. Martini is sleepwalking, running, believing he is immersed in a very nasty gun battle alone, thousands of feet in the air and very, very frightened. You, of course, know the sequence I mean?'

James is confident that he does, despite the slow rush of blood he can feel building in his cheeks. He has read the play between homework assignments, sitting at the kitchen table as his mother fussed and cleaned.

'What's that you're reading?' his mother had asked.

'Nothing.'

He had looked at her. He knew that mood, that brittle hung-over mood. She and Sully had been out until late the night before. They had woken him up when they got back. All day she had been in bad form, giving James that I'm-watching-you stare.

'Don't give me that! What is it? You've been stuck in it for hours.' She grabbed the play and began to read it. He made a lunge for it but she moved away. 'Is this to do with your English studies?'

'Sort of.'

'Either it is or it isn't.'

'Mr Shannon asked me to be in it.'

'In what? In this?'

He nods. She hands back the play. 'You mean appear in it?'

'Yeah.'

She doesn't say anything, just looks at him. Then she says, 'I'm not happy about it.'

'Why?'

'I'm not.'

'Why, Mum?'

'I'm your mother and I'm not happy. Mothers get to say things like that. OK?'

He had gathered up his books and stormed out of the kitchen. His mother had followed him to the doorway shouting after him: 'I don't want you reading that thing. I don't like that Shannon one, I never did. He's far too smooth for my liking. Did you hear what I said?'

After that he had brought the text to bed with him and used a torch to pore over it in case his mother caught him. It was there that he had first glimpsed the world of the play. As the night had worn on he grew bored of the text and threw shadows on the wall by the bed. It was there that the characters had begun to live.

McMurphy, Shannon's character, had loomed before him, in hard dark lines. Chief Bowden had lurched across the wall, his arms and legs long timbers of shadow. Billy Babbit, the stuttering kid of the asylum, was a shake of the torch, so that its spilling light seemed to dance him into life. Then suddenly, with the force of a dark fist, his character Martini had come to life. It had thrust itself across the wall like a big black jigsaw bird, its beak James's trembling knuckles, its eyes two dark holes that seemed to drink the light.

'When you are quite ready, Lav—'

Before Shannon can even complete his surname, James turns in his seat and, reaching into the fireplace, grabs the dead crow. In one movement he lifts it above him, raining ash all over Chin Chin's head. In his mind he sees his character perched in a helicopter gunship and the dead crow's wings its churning blades. With the bird now rotating above his head James runs round the rehearsal room shouting, 'Bandits at three o'clock! Bandits at three o'clock! May Day! May Day!'

The two women scream.

'Ratatat! Ratatat! Ratatat! I'm hit! I'm hit!'

The bird makes an eerie swishing sound in his hand. A hush falls across the room as he runs to and fro, the wings of the dead bird flapping above his head. Eventually exhausted he slumps to his knees. 'May Day . . . This is Martini. May Day.'

The crow's glazed eye looks up at him, and feathers float down all around him. Slowly, he finds himself back in the room once more. He looks around him. He sees their stunned faces. He wants to tell them about the big jigsaw bird that had flown out of the shadows on to his bedroom wall the other night. He wants to say that it had seemed right to use the crow. He wants to say many things. He wants to understand the roar that had risen in him as he had run round the room, the hard bright anger that had bolted from his gut. He wants to tell them that his father had died for Ireland, and that Ireland didn't give a shit.

'Sssh.'

That was what Teezy had said when she had secretly given him the photograph, her finger raised to her lips.

'Here . . . your father died for Ireland . . . sssh . . .'

'Sssh.'

He gets to his feet. The room is silent. Patricia peers from behind her fingers, Kerry's hands are over her mouth. Cathal Murphy's Paisley cravat is now hanging from his fingers. Chin Chin is nodding, a smile gleaming in his eye. Mr Shannon takes a deep breath, his eyes narrowing in concentration. 'Hmmm . . . I think the accent needs a little work, Lavery, but full marks for the inventive use of available props.'

When the rehearsal is over Shannon asks James to stay behind. They sit in silence for a moment or two, James gazing fiercely at his shoes, not daring to meet Shannon's gaze.

'I'm not going to bite, Lavery.'

'Yes, sir.'

'Sean . . . Call me Sean.'

'Sean.'

'It was very imaginative, what you did earlier.'

'Yes, sir . . . Sean.'

'Don't be so hard on yourself, Lavery. You did nothing wrong, far from it. You used this.' He taps his forehead and winks. 'Now, off you go. See you on the morrow.'

'Thank you, sir . . . Sean.'

'No – thank *you*, James.'

As he steps out into the night air, his chest swells with pride as he makes his way up Joseph Street. As he rounds the corner on to Hill Street he taps his forehead with his fingers in self-congratulation.

Death by Being Dropped into Ireland's Greedy Endless Mouth

The big black jigsaw bird has me. I can see the scuttling of the people below me, their small, scurrying shapes bumping and jostling each other. Above me I feel the heavy swoosh of wind from the bird's wing thrusts; I feel the steel bite of its claws along the run of my back. I can smell the stench of old carrion from its warm, sickly breath. Higher and higher I am lifted until the ground below is a distant memory. I think of the look of surprise on my mother's face when the bird swooped and gathered me in its vice-like grip, its large head cutting skywards. I remember how her scream broke the crisp morning air, and her hands flailed at the departing bird as if she was trying to deter a troublesome wasp. I heard my name fade on her lips, and I was sure I caught the glint'of a falling tear.

I am not afraid, only puzzled. I had thought that the big jackdaw was my friend and I cannot understand why he is suddenly so aggressive with me. Clouds come and go like floury fists. Small thrusts and swirls of air play and tug at the soft flesh of my neck, and my feet bob and tick on the ends of my legs, like fishing floats. At first I recognise the countryside below me, and grin as I see my school rush by, its playing-fields like long green tablets, glistening in the morning sun. I even believe I see my aunt Teezy's house, small grey puffs of smoke rising from its short fat chimneys, and I wave. But then the countryside gets darker, and the wind fresher, and small dots of falling hail sting my eyes. We are flying through heavy, dense mist and I lose all sense of time. All I can hear is the swooshing beat of the bird's wings and the loud patter of my heart.

Suddenly, below me, the mist parts and I can see a mountain rising up to meet us, and in the middle of this mountain's peak is a large foul-smelling mouth. Ireland's mouth. I realise with horror that I am going to be fed to it. All around the fringe of the mountain's peak I see dismembered limbs and old bones: they cover the ground below me like forgotten stones. As the bird drops me, I realise that this is where all the young men of Ireland go; this is where my father went. As I hurtle through the air, the mountain opens its mouth and I see the blood and guts of a nation's men rushing to meet me.

6. *The Bomb*

The following Saturday morning a bomb goes off in the town. James and his mother had driven the three miles from the estate, and were on the small roundabout at Carrick Street when they heard the blast. James thought it sounded like a giant punching a huge fist into the Earth's mantle. The buildings that lined the street vibrated momentarily and some of the shop windows spewed broken glass on to the pavement. Ahead at the top of the street, just where it rounded into Canal Street, James can see a white puff of smoke rise; it reminds him of the knot of smoke that the Vatican uses to announce a new pope. A shop alarm sounds, its discordant wail puncturing the eerie silence that had settled in the aftermath of the explosion.

That means his town will be on the news tonight, James thinks. He can see the reporter standing before the tangled mass of shop frontage and buckled vehicles, cement dust falling like papery rain into the camera lens.

Two cars ahead of them have collided, the front of one pushed back on itself like a discarded paper cup. The drivers stand by the doors of their vehicles, a lost look on their faces, like children whose sweet ration has just been stopped. James's mother hasn't moved since the blast occurred. Her hands have left the steering-wheel and frozen midway to her face. She is gaping as if someone has just skewered her through the chest.

For what seems an age, the traffic, with its cargo of shoppers and children, sits where it is, the ball of smoke ahead seeping like squid ink into the sky. He hears the whine of sirens somewhere behind him, and turns to see a phalanx of blue lights fighting their way through the backed-up traffic. James looks again to his mother, and notices that her body is shuddering, and that two long tears are working their way down her cheeks.

Suddenly a fire-engine fills their rear-view mirror, like a colossal red whale, its siren squealing. The driver inches it closer and closer to their car, pressing the horn with hard, sharp bangs of his hand. James can see the co-driver wave his arms, furiously gesturing for them to get out of the way. 'Mum, please . . .' he says.

His mother grabs the steering-wheel and shunts the

car out of the way, mounting the pavement with an ungainly thump. They watch the fire-engine stream past, followed by two police Land Rovers and a couple of army Saracens. Other drivers take advantage of the sudden slipstream of free road to shoot through, leaving James and his mother stuck, tilted on the high pavement.

His mother parks at the other end of town in a rundown car park, squeezing the car between two vans, cursing loudly as she bumps the side of one, then looking around nervously to see if anyone has noticed. For a moment she sits there, her hands laid out flat, knuckle up on the rim of the steering-wheel.

He wonders if anyone has been killed in the explosion, and about the threshold they might have passed across as they died. What was it like, he wondered. Did the souls of the victims leave the earth as they passed over? Did the sky peel back like ripped plastic sheeting and did their spirits hurtle through the opened heavens into the blackness of space? There, did the souls orbit each other, like fireflies, in the starry wastes of the universe?

'I've a couple of things to do,' his mother says.

'Right.'

'Will you be all right?'

'What do you mean?'

'I don't want you going near that mess over there.'

'I'm not a baby.'

'That's not what I meant.'

'I'll be fine.'

'You're not listening,' she says.

'What?'

'Stay close to this part of the town. Do you hear me?'

'Yes, I hear you.'

'Look at me! I said, look at me.'

He looks at her. She seems so lost, so frightened. 'OK,' he says.

'Right. I'll meet you back here in an hour,' his mother says, and gives him a fifty pence piece.

He begins to cross the small bridge that spans the canal, heading towards the shops on the other side. He looks back towards the car park and watches his mother cross the road. He sees her pause outside Campbell's bar. Then she casts a quick look back in the direction of the car park before she is swallowed by the dark of the bar's doorway. So that was why she didn't want him with her: she wanted her booze. Suddenly all the compassion he had felt for her leaves him. If she doesn't care, then neither does he. It's that simple.

Go on, he thinks. Go on, drown yourself.

The billow of smoke from the explosion has subsided: it now throws up only faint fumes, like the embers of a dying cigar. Using it as a guide, James begins to work his way to the site of the bomb, his legs pumping down the streets. As he gets closer he can smell charred wood and incinerated rubber, and hear the shouts of the men from the emergency services. People pass him by, their faces pale with fear. He feels as if he is running into the opened mouth of hell. He can see the beginnings of fires, on the rims of car tyres, licking at the wooden frames of doorways.

Suddenly he feels something whip by his ear, and sees what he thinks is a small tick of light, or a firefly hover in the line of his vision, then flit furiously down the street away from him. As it passes it warms his heart, and he can feel long fingers of heat work along his gut and a smile begin on his lips.

Ahead, he can see a line of RUC men. They straddle the mouth of the street where the bomb has gone off, ushering frantic figures through their human cordon, shouting for everyone to clear the area. He looks for the dot of light but it has gone, as quickly and as mysteriously as it arrived. He tells himself that it was nothing but sunlight bouncing off car glass or a shop window.

He slips down a side-street that runs parallel to Hill Street and the site of the bomb, avoiding the line of policemen, hoping to grab a quick look at the devastation.

He rounds the corner and is facing on to the middle of Hill Street. He stands and looks down the alleyway and sees a car lying in pieces on the ground. Behind it, the figures of two people are staggering back and forth across the mouth of the alleyway. One, a man in his forties, is shirtless, and his vest hangs in torn lips of cloth from his body. His left arm is bloodied and the left side of his face is matted with dirt and blood. He shuffles aimlessly across the alleyway, his arms weaving strange loops in the air, his mouth uttering soft moans of protest. The other person is a young woman. At one point she sits on the torn ridge of the car door and rests her head tenderly in her hands, her bone-thin shoulders quivering, her hands dotted with blood.

In the background people stream past, their heads fixed downwards, their limbs tightly held, as if they still wore the roar of the blast on their bodies. Firemen drag huge hoses, their heads upturned in the direction of a rogue blaze. Soldiers fill the sides of the main street, their short, spiked guns half cocked on their arms.

A man stands at the beginning of the alleyway. James hasn't seen him arrive, hasn't seen him round the corner, and the sight of him brings a shiver to his skin. He seems to be cut from the dense cloth of the alleyway's shadows, and so tall that James has to crane his neck to get a look at his face. The deep navy pinstriped suit looks familiar, as does the fist-sized knot of his tie. He is strangely untouched, his suit immaculate, his hair finely neatened, his clear eyes gazing unwaveringly at James.

It is the man from the photograph Teezy had told him

was his father. It is the man of half-remembered fragments, the man he had been told was dead.

James steps forward. The man seems to beckon him. The noise and panic of the morning are falling away, and he feels as if he is walking across a shimmering sheet of light towards the man's hands. He opens his mouth to speak, but the words leave him like mute birds, flapping away into the smoky air. Still the man beckons, his eyes filled with the soft passion of someone who has waited a long, long time.

Perhaps he is alive: perhaps he has secretly lived his life and is now returning to reclaim him. Perhaps Teezy lied to him. Perhaps he has lived a life of quiet patience, biding his time before coming back for him.

As if released from a strong, invisible web, his body starts forward. His legs move towards the figure. A hard cry falls from his lips. As he shoots forward he snags his foot on a piece of thrown car metal. He sees the ground of the alleyway rush to meet him. He feels the breath leave his body in a winded gasp, and he scrabbles desperately to right himself.

'Shit.'

Slowly he pushes his knees up beneath his body and tries to catch his breath, then attempts to stand. The hand, when it grabs him, feels hard. He can feel its strong yank work its way through his body. He tells himself that it is only his father's eager insistence to hold him after all these years, his desire to look his son in the face once more. As he is pulled to his feet, he lifts his head to meet the strong, fearless gaze of his father, to look deep into his eyes and to thank God for his return.

'What the fuck do you think you're at, wee boy?'

The hand that is holding him belongs to the arm of a fireman. His father, only moments ago so vivid, is nowhere to be seen.

'What the fuck is your problem, son? Have you a death-wish?'

The man in the alleyway has gone and the fireman frogmarches him away from the bomb site. He tries to protest but the fireman tells him to be quiet or he'll snap his neck like a pencil. He tells him that a second incendiary has just been phoned in, and it is his duty to see the area cleared.

When they reach the safety of the next street, the fireman lets go of him, and glowers. 'Now, get the fuck away from here.'

But James doesn't hear him: his eyes are searching for the man in the pinstriped suit who had filled the neck of the alleyway only moments before.

He meets his mother back at the car. Her mood is tougher, spikier.

'Where were you?'

'Down the town.'

'Where? What happened your clothes? I'm asking you a question!'

He doesn't answer her. He watches as she fumbles to put the key into the lock of the driver's door, her hair falling across her face as she curses quietly to herself. Then she stops. He can see her shoulders rise and fall. She lifts her head and looks him straight in the eye. 'I told you not to go there. What happened?'

'I fell.'

'Fell where? Fell where? I asked you to stay in this part of the town. Did you not hear me? You promised me, young man.'

'I didn't go far.'

'Are you trying to get yourself killed?'

'I saw him.'

'Who?'

'My father. I felt him . . . and then I saw him. In Castle Street, in the alleyway.'

She snaps her eyes down, away from his. He can hear the jiggle of her car keys in her hand.

'I'm sorry?' she says, still not looking at him.

This time when he says it his voice is softer, more reasonable: 'I said I saw him . . . Daddy. I saw him back there in the alleyway.'

'Is this some kind of joke, James?' She's looking at him again. Her eyes are moist and hard. 'Get in the car.'

'No. First I felt him like a firefly. Then I saw him.'

'What do you mean, you "felt" him? What the fuck do you mean, you "felt" him?'

'I felt him.'

'You're doing this deliberately, aren't you? You want me mad! You want me insane! Get in the car! Get in the friggin' car.'

'No.'

'Get in the car when I tell you.'

'No. He was wearing a pinstripe suit. Mum, I felt him.'

'You'll feel my friggin' hand.'

As she strides round the back of the car to get at him she snags her hip on the rear wing. 'Fuck! What are you trying to do to me?'

'Nothing. I'm not trying to do anything.'

He feels her hands on him, pawing and pulling, grabbing at his collar. She hits him with her open palms. He brings his arms above his head and waits for the flailing to stop. She opens the car door, shoves him inside and, for a moment, stands guard by the passenger door, then marches round to the driver's side. She gets in, fires the engine and rips the car into reverse. 'Did Teezy put you up to this? Has she been filling your head?'

'No.'

'Sometimes I think I'd be better off without any of you. You're all fucking liars.'

A passing car blares its horn as they make a sideways weave, briefly crossing the middle line of the road.

'I'd drown the lot of you – drown you in your own fucking lies.' She bangs her hand on the horn, and almost without him realising it his hand shoots out to rest on her arm to calm her.

'Don't touch me! You make me sick – you all make me sick.'

As soon as they reach home he bolts, running headlong for the fields that border the small estate, hearing the cries of his mother. When he looks back he sees her swaying in their doorway.

'I felt him! I felt him!' he shouts back at her.

The wind sweeps away his words, steals them from his mouth and hurls them heavenwards. He imagines them climbing, pushing through the cold air, wriggling through the clouds and bursting through to where a small colony of fireflies hovers together in the far reaches of outer space.

Letter to a Firefly

James Lavery
My Bedroom
Night

I believe in you. She doesn't, but I do. I know she didn't mean to hurt me. Please don't think too badly of her. Is it cold where you are? Are the days endless? Do you think of me? Was it chance that you came by? I've just started rehearsing a play. I'm enjoying it very much. I'm playing a character called Martini. He has an imaginary friend and he spends his time holding conversations with him. There was a huge bomb in the town today. I don't know if anyone died, but maybe you know better than I do. Was that you, that hot swish of light that flew by me? I think it was. Mum went crazy when I told her. She hasn't done that for a long, long time. She misses you, I know. She misses you.

I felt you. Today I felt you like a hot sun. It made me feel safe. It made me feel warm. Do you have any friends up there? No women friends, though, I don't think Mum would like that. We all miss you. Teezy misses you. I see it in her eyes when she thinks no one is looking. It's like a tiredness that sits in the middle of them, like a small cloud. She used to tell me that you died for Ireland. I don't think Ireland cares: it just carries on as usual. Sometimes I lie in bed at night and imagine that I'm flying with you, two bright little dots of light travelling together, watching stars and planets whiz by.

When I was smaller I believed that you had gone away to be an astronaut, that something had gone wrong and you couldn't get back. I know now that

*you are something better, something that doesn't
need a spaceship. I know that you can see everything. You and your friends (do you have any?) are
like small gods hovering everywhere, seeing how
we're doing. I perform different deaths sometimes,
for my friends. Most of the time, though, I just
think them. I try to imagine what it would be like
one minute to be me and then the next something
else, a firefly like you. Is that what happens? Maybe
not. I don't know.*

   *I feel strange, cold, because suddenly I don't
think you're there. That happens a lot. It makes me
feel stupid. You are there, aren't you? Dad?*

Love, James

7. The Fight

Sully and James's mother are fighting, they are at break-fast downstairs. James is still in bed: he can hear them from beneath the blankets he has pulled over his head. He can hear his mother's voice tighten as it is raised, like the sound her car clutch makes when she mistimes it. It is early: light is breaking in long lines in the sky.

He closes his eyes as the fight moves from the kitchen into the living room. He car hear the force of Sully's walk ringing through the house. He can imagine him, his eyes darting wildly, and his pocked cheekbones red with anger.

He can imagine his mother. He can see her pursuing him, spitting accusations, her hands drawing diagrams of betrayal in the cold morning air.

He decides to get up and get out. Moving quickly, he dresses. He goes to the bedroom door and puts his ear to it. Slowly he turns the handle and pulls the door to him a fraction. The shouting has subsided. He goes towards the bathroom, carrying his shoes and socks, moving with guarded stealth on the landing carpet.

He rounds the top of the stairs. His mother and Sully are seated on the settee below him. His mother's back is to him: her lime green cardigan seems pulled and grabbed at, her head is lowered, her shoulders tensed.

'Fucker, Sully . . . bastard, fucker, pig . . .' He mouths the words, each one a hiss, and pummels the air with short-pulled punches. 'Fucker, Sully . . . bastard, fucker, pig.' He bends himself double to get a better purchase on the blows, so they almost swing back into his own face. 'Bastard! Bastard!'

He reaches the bathroom, closes the door behind him and finishes dressing. He pulls the window open, grimaces as it scrapes, then grabs the outer sill and pulls himself out. Using his hands, he levers himself so that he sits precariously on the outside ledge, gripping the window runners, his legs knocking against the outside wall. Gingerly his fingers feel for the drainpipe, and he inches towards it. Using both arms, he pulls himself into a hug with it and descends.

At about ten feet from the ground he throws a glance below him, then pushes away. He lands with a crunch on the gravel, and takes a moment to fix his collar and tie, then checks his satchel. He looks around: the world seems vaporous and magical. A shudder quickens in him, and he starts towards the woods.

'Bastard Sully . . . Sully bastard. Bastard Sully.'

He enters the woods at a gallop, then slows to a walk. He likes the woods, with their cathedral of trees and their small pools of stillness. He breaks off a long stripling and runs his palms along its knotty shanks. He puts it to his shoulder, one hand on the trigger, the other midway on the stock.

He swings the rifle round, searching for danger, his finger poised to strike at any moment, his right eye squinted shut as he inches forward, his feet placed, his ears listening for the click of a mine trigger or the rustle of an enemy patrol. A pigeon breaks from the canopy above him, its wings clapping loudly in its panic to clear the trees.

'Enemy at three o'clock!' He screams the words in his most forceful German accent. He has always identified with the Germans. Teezy had often spoken of the special regard Hitler had for Ireland, offering De Valera freedom from the British in return for co-operation. In games of war, in the playground or on the way back from school, it was a real problem to find a 'Brit' among his friends. Arguments would rage as boy after boy refused, saying that if it came to it they would rather be a 'wop Italian' or a 'sneaky Jap', anything but a 'Brit'.

Suddenly he smiles to himself as he sees Sully's face loom into view, his head bloated like a football, a large cigar clamped between his teeth. Sully as Winston Churchill, Sully as fat Sir Winston Churchill. 'We shall fight them on the beaches, fat smug Sir Sully Churchill . . .'

The bird is almost free of the ceiling of the forest: he snaps his rifle up and tracks it, his finger lightly poised on the trigger.

'Die, *Herr Englander* Sully Churchill, *die –*'

The bullets fly in a torrent. His shoulder bucks at their force.

'Bam, bam, bam! Die, Sir Sully Pig Dog . . . Die . . . Bam, bam!'

The British plane containing the fat head of Sully is dispatched; he sees it spiral into the trees and imagines Sully's body consumed by flames.

'No mercy for the *Englanders*. No mercy.'

Another pigeon breaks loose of the branches. He wheels to catch it in his sights and stops dead, the blood draining from his face, the stick in his hands pointing straight between the eyes of a real British paratrooper. For a moment they stay that way, until the soldier reaches out and takes the stick from James.

The patrol walks him the short distance across the field and returns him to his mother. They search the house. James can hear the thud of their heavy boots as they move from room to room, upending beds and clothes. The one who caught him stays in the kitchen with them, eyeing them, his fingers tapping nervously on his gun. He can be no more than twenty, and his face is stained with camouflage paint, his helmet webbed with netting.

Sully takes out his Old Holborn and rolls a cigarette, throwing the tobacco pouch on to the table. James's mother pats Sully's arm. He pulls it away and looks at the young soldier as he brings the gummed paper to his lips, never taking his eyes off him as his head lolls from side to side. He seals the cigarette and lights it, slaps the lighter down on the table. Eventually the other soldiers return.

'Well, how many bombs did you find?'

The sergeant steps forward. He is older than the others. He clears his throat as if he were a vicar addressing a congregation weary of the sermon. 'Sorry, madam, but it's policy. A house like this in this area is to be searched. It's an area of known sympathies.'

'Leave my house,' she says.

The soldiers depart. James watches through the window as they merge with the fields, their uniformed figures melting slowly into the landscape.

Sully gets up, joins James at the window and inhales his cigarette hungrily. 'Look at those fuckers . . . If I had my way . . .' Then he stares at James. 'Know what I'm saying?'

James doesn't reply but moves away from him to sit at the kitchen table.

James's mother begins to clear up, stacking the breakfast plates in the sink, snapping the tap on with a hard twist of her hand, running the hot water. She grabs the dishcloth and shakes it in brisk, flapping movements, the pedal bin open beneath it. Then she wipes the table. Suddenly she stops. Sully continues to look out at the fields, his hands now thrust into his back pockets. James's mother throws up her head and eyes her son. 'What the bloody hell do you think you were doing? How did you get out?'

'The bathroom window.'

'Jesus, you could have frigging broken something! Why? Why?'

Sully slowly turns to look at James. 'James, you're doing my head in, son.'

James doesn't say anything but returns his mother's look. She walks over to her son. 'All this stuff . . . this dreaming of yours . . . It's not right. I haven't slept a bloody wink since last week . . . since the day in the town.'

'That's not my fault,' he says.

'She's not friggin' saying that! Jesus!' Sully has joined in.

'Sully, let me handle it, OK?'

'OK, OK . . . whatever. You're both as thick as that hill out there.'

'Sully, haven't you caused enough trouble?'

He sees Sully bite his lip and wheel away from them to resume his window vigil, pulling angrily on his cigarette.

'James.'

'Yeah.'

'Come on, son . . .'

'What?'

'Stop all this.'

'Stop all what?'

Sully wheels back and advances slowly into the middle of the kitchen, angrily stubbing out his cigarette on a saucer. 'Listen, kid, there's no fucking man in a suit, no friggin' firebugs – or pieces of effing light, OK? Get it into your thick skull. You're driving us all to distraction, for fuck's sake.'

'Sully, no – Sully.' His mother tries to stop him.

'Pieces of bugs, for fuck's sake – you're cracked, you're frightening your mammy.'

'Sully, that's enough.'

'No, excuse me a fucking second here, Ann. I've had enough – I know what I'd do with him.'

'Yeah, Sully. That's your answer for everything, isn't it?'

So that's why they were fighting. That's why the two of them had been at each other's throats. He was the prey. Sully wanted a hold of him, but he had to go through James's mother to get his hands on him.

The Fight

An hour later Sully runs James to school. They take the back roads, listening to the odd swish of puddles beneath the tyres. He watches Sully's hands riding the steering-wheel, flipping it this way and that. They trundle down Nurse's Hill, and join the long procession of school traffic. Sully reaches into the pocket of his jeans and pulls out his tobacco. He throws the pouch into James's lap. 'Roll me one, and pack it loose, do you hear? Go on.'

Sully sneaks sidelong glances at him, and when they stop at a set of traffic-lights watches him more openly. 'Lightly . . . That's it . . . Roll it lightly, otherwise it'll be as tight as a monkey's arse.'

James's forefingers and thumbs work the paper and tobacco. Then he brings it to his lips and licks the paper's gum, for a moment believing that every flick of his tongue is bleeding poison on to the paper, a deadly Sully-killing poison.

He hands over the cigarette to Sully, who inspects it, holding it out in front of his eyes, the cigarette lying horizontally across his bunched fingertips. The lights have changed and the backed-up cars behind them rev their engines in gathering impatience. Sully is not to be hurried.

A horn sounds. James shifts uneasily in his seat, and throws a quick look over his shoulder: the horns are hooting now with more urgency. He knows that Sully is making a point. He's letting him know who's boss in the troubled mess of their small world. Sully now has the cigarette between his lips and lights it, his other hand shifting the van into first gear as the lights go to amber. The first billow of smoke comes from his lips as the van moves left on to High Street, leaving the traffic behind him stuck on another red light, their horns blaring in fury.

'Good cigarette, kiddo. Good draw.'

They arrive at the school. Sully parks, pulling hard on the handbrake. They sit there for a moment watching the stream of boys arrive. Sully finishes his cigarette, drawing on it right down to the nub, his mouth pursed to get at the last dregs of nicotine. He stubs it aggressively in the ashtray. James can sense him looking at him. Father Boyle stands watch outside the heavy oak door of the school, separating any boys who are too boisterous and pushing them inside the doorway with a strong thrust of his hand.

'Jimmy . . . I . . . You're a good kid, you mean well,' Sully says.

Carefully James places his hand on the door handle, letting it rest there, feeling a throb in his wrist.

'It's just . . . Listen, it's just your mum's . . . delicate.'

But James is not interested. He opens the van door and steps down, his satchel clattering from the seat on to the tarmac. He retrieves it hurriedly, stuffs his exercise book and pens back inside, and walks round the front of the van as Sully fires it into life. As he passes Sully winds down his window, catching James half-way to the school door. 'Hey, kiddo, don't let that monkey over there fuck you about.'

With a toot of the horn Sully speeds away down the school drive, his free arm waving a triumphant farewell from the driver's window.

'The bastard,' James mutters to himself.

'Master Lavery.'

He turns to see Father Boyle bearing down on him. He takes James's earlobe between his forefinger and thumb and steers him towards the school entrance. On tiptoe, James complies, his ear stretched in pain.

'If that layabout was a blood relation of yours both you and he would be in serious trouble . . . Now, about your day, my boy.'

The Last Moments of a True Believer

I had a feeling they were both spies. I didn't fully realise it until they rounded on me this morning in the kitchen of Gestapo Headquarters. All the pretence on their faces fell away, and I saw them as they really are: liars, thieves and, worst of all, traitorous spies. But although I had always distrusted him, I thought that somewhere she still believed in me, believed in our cause. Unfortunately that was

not the case, and when I saw her betray me in front
of him this morning, I knew the Fatherland was in
jeopardy as soon as she began to cry those false
tears, those whiny, poor-me tears.

You told me always to be on the lookout, to be
wary of those closest, but I never for a moment
thought my own mother, your wife, would side with
the enemy. You always said that the English were
never to be trusted, that they were the most cunning
race on the planet, even more so than our
inscrutable allies, the Japanese. You said betrayal
was everywhere, and today I saw it in the harsh
eyes of Commandant Sully, and grasped that he was
a traitor to his backbone, and that over the past
few years he had quietly worked his evil propa-
ganda on my poor, deluded mother.

She would rather have his love, have his traitor's
hands on her skin, than the one true love of a son,
and the undying love of our Glorious Fatherland,
for which you gave your only life, dear Father. You
see I knew this morning, even before the incident in
the Gestapo kitchen when he lost his temper with
me. I saw his face in the cockpit of one of the
English planes I shot down. It was then that I
understood, and I felt such a fool.

I also know he has poisoned me. It occurred in
the staff vehicle as he was taking me to my next

assignment. He asked me to roll a cigarette for him. It was only as I was handing it to him that I realised with a shudder that the gum on the paper was laced with a deadly barbiturate. Before I go, I am determined to unmask them to the world, to bring the full vengeance of the Third Reich down on their treacherous heads. I look forward to seeing you, my father, in our glorious German Heaven. I feel a cold shadow move across my heart, I know it won't be long. I have less time than I thought . . . I have so much to do . . . Farewell and hello, dear Father.

Your son
General James von Lavery

8. Plug and the Big 'Ammer

James is standing in the history corridor with Plug. They are waiting for the class before them to leave. They lean nonchalantly against the wall, killing time, watching their classmates assemble around them in the vague semblance of a queue.

'Well?'

'Well what?'

'Did you go?'

'Yeah.'

'Well?'

'I heard that bit, Plug.'

Plug is his best friend, called Plug because he has small ears that remind people of the character from the *Beano*. They had first met a few years before when they had both arrived at St Patrick's. His father owns a couple of small hardware shops, one in the town and another across the border in Dundalk. He has three sisters, each a tiny feminine replica of him, with the same flawless openness to their faces. James has visited his house many times. He loves the fuss Plug's mother makes of him, and the gentle way his father smiles at him whenever he arrives.

'Did you go to Shannon's effing rehearsal?'

'Why don't you just come out and say it, Plug?'

'What?'

'Fuck – not "eff", not "frig", fuck. Fuck. Fuck.'

'Eff off, Lavery.'

'No.'

'Eff off – there.'

'You still didn't say it. Why can't you curse like a normal fucking human, Plug?'

'Eff you.'

'No, fuck me. Fuck me.'

'What was that, son?'

'Sorry, sir?'

Mr Hogben is standing before them. He is the head of the history department, a small man with rat-like features, and wavy hair that spills about his ears and face. He constantly fidgets with it, splaying his long fingers and pushing them through it, then patting and tapping it into shape. 'What were you saying with such vehemence, young Lavery?'

'Nothing, sir.'

'I hope so, son, because if it was what I thought at first it was, there'd be no bleeding skin left on your hands.'

Hogben is a Cockney, the only English teacher in the school; as a consequence he is viewed with distrust by the pupils. He is a passionate West Ham supporter, and if a pupil has any sense he learns quickly to become one too because, come the bell for history on Monday morning, God help any boy who takes private glee from a West Ham defeat. He has a volcanic temper that erupts almost without warning, especially if he has taken a dislike to a pupil, and most especially if he suspects a boy wishes ill towards his beloved Hammers. James and Plug watch as Hogben runs his small ratty eyes over the rest of the students in their scattered queue.

'All right, my boys. One all against the namby-pamby Spurs on Saturday . . . So don't bleedin' push it today. In you go – and, Lavery . . .'

'Yes, sir?'

'Who do we adore?'

'The Hammers, sir.'

'No, my son, no. The 'Ammers, son – no H. Now say it.'

'The 'Ammers, sir.'

'Complete the following. Bobby who, son?'

'Moore, sir.'

'I'll make bleedin' 'Ammers out of you lot yet. In you

go – and no lip from any of you or my hand'll be on your faces, you gammy lot.'

That day at lunchtime, between hot gulps of apple crumble and lumpy custard, Plug continues his interrogation of James. 'Come on, spill it.'

'They were weird.'

'Told you. They're all weird, that lot.'

'No, you didn't.'

'Yes, I effin' did.'

'Bollocks.'

'Actors.'

'But they're not actors.'

'That's what I mean. They want to be, which makes them even more actory.'

As he says 'actory', Plug waves his arms in front of his face as if he was drawing big flowery clouds in the air, knocking a neighbouring boy's spoonful of dessert into his teeth.

'Hey, watch what you're doing, McGowan.'

'Oh, eff off, small fry.'

That night as he lies in bed she comes to stand by him. She hasn't done it for a long time, but he knows how it will follow. She will stand there, watching him sleep, watching the soft up-down of his breathing. This time, though, for the first time he sits upright in the bed and stares back. 'Mum.'

'Sorry, son. I thought you were asleep.'

'No.'

'Do you want some company?'

She sits softly on the end of his bed, her hands resting in her lap. So this is it, he thinks, a truce. A truce by moonlight. She reaches out to touch the side of his face. He feels her hand settle on his cheek. 'My beautiful young man.'

He sees the burn of her eyes looking at him in the grainy moonlight, holding him, claiming him.

'Whose are you?'

'Yours.'

'Yes, mine.'

'Mum, you OK?'

Her hand is still on his face. It makes him feel uncomfortable. She nods, her eyes never leaving his. It reminds him of that walk he had made many years before when she had called herself his queen and he had danced with her. Long ago when the sherry had shone in her glass, years before when he had first heard his dead father's name, and she had shot it down, killed it as it had left Teezy's lips, stamped it out as it had struggled to be heard.

'Budge over,' she says.

After a moment he parts the bedclothes and offers her his bed. He watches as she swings her legs up from the carpet. He feels them enter the bed and search for the warmth of his feet. They spread their cool power through the bed. He feels her head land softly on the bone of his chest, and her hair spill across it.

'My beautiful young man.' She says it again. This time she makes a tiny snuffle with her mouth, like a small resting animal glad to have come across warmth. 'Tell your mum you love her.'

He can smell the evening's drink on her, its stale force hanging in a sickly cloud above them.

'I'm tired, Mum.'

'Tell her.'

She has lifted her head so that her breath is running into his, so that her lips are a finger's breadth from his. Closer up, her eyes have a trance-like pall, and he can see the dark, cavernous rings beneath them.

'Tell your mother you love her.'

'I love you.'

'How's the play coming?' she asks suddenly.

'All right . . . I like it.'

'Are you an actor, then?'

'I don't know . . . Do you want to come and see it? When we do it?'

There's a pause as she thinks about what he has just asked. Then she lowers her head back to his chest and says quietly, 'You're all right, son, it's not my thing. I'd feel funny around that lot.'

'OK.'

It's no surprise. She hates change. She hates anything that takes him out of her watchful domain. He knows that. There is a pause and then she says quietly, 'Good boy . . . Now sleep with Mummy . . . Sleep sound with Mummy and all your dreams will be white and free . . . And in the morning, no more stories, no more fireflies . . .' Her voice breaks on 'fireflies' and sticks, and her hand tightens on his stomach, squeezing, scratching at the flesh it finds there. He can feel her nails pinch, and her body shiver. In a moment she is asleep, snores rising from her like a car ticking over.

'Conn?'

She says it softly in her sleep. He lies there and thinks of himself beginning in her belly all those years before, a fleck, no bigger than a thumbnail. He thinks of himself walled into her, while on the outside he imagines his father standing before her, his hand to her belly, caressing the thought of him there. He imagines the pride in her eyes for the thread of life she carries beneath her heart. He closes his eyes and pushes himself back into her womb. He imagines himself floating through the water-ways of her heart, deeper, into the pit of her, and he brings hate with him to the place where he began. He doesn't want to, but it flares in him; it lights his way. He brings his anger; he brings his rage, at her, at the world, at the father who is gone. He brings his loathing of Sully. He brings murder to the history of himself.

Letter from an Unborn Child

> *Yet to be named James Lavery*
> *Yet to live in: 11 Erin Grove*
> *Carickburren*

Mother,
Kill me. I don't want to be born. It is better this way,
better not to trouble you with me. I can see the future
from your womb. I can see the pain of the long hours
of my childhood, when your eyes will meet mine and
sorrow will rise there. Can you hear me, Mother? I
will say this as you sleep, as my father's hand rubs my
shape in your belly. Kill me. Tell God it was my idea.
That way maybe nothing will happen, maybe things
will be different. That way I won't know anything. I
won't see anything. I won't feel anything.

You see, I know your dreams. I see what you are.
I can see what God has planned from here, and I
know I will forget it when I am in your arms.
Maybe if I go God will be happy with that and
won't take Dad. That's the best thing to do because
I know how much you will miss him, and our lives
will be dead anyway.

I am only a dot at the minute. No one is going to notice if a dot disappears. The universe is so big that I could just go back to where I came from and quietly tell God that you didn't want me and that it was better that way. Maybe then Dad will live and I could come back another time.

Kind regards
Your yet-to-be-named son, James Lavery

9. Al Pacino

Rehearsals are now something that he looks forward to, expectantly counting the hours and the days until Monday and Wednesday evenings come round. After school he runs the mile or so to the rehearsal rooms, like a child rushing downstairs on Christmas morning.

Mr Shannon has augmented the cast with recruits from the local amateur operatic society, and punters from the local GAA club. Most are used to fill out the ward scenes, and are required to do no more than shuffle to and fro across the playing space. One, Jarlath McAllister, is also the cast driver, in charge of ferrying the actors to the opera house, come the time. He is a wide, squat man, with large muscles that bulge from beneath his caramel-coloured leather jacket. He has taken a shine to James, laughing every time the boy launches into the Italian accent he is using for Martini, shaking his head and wagging his finger at him.

James loves the feverishness of the rehearsal room. He loves the freedom, and the gentle ribbing of the actors. Shannon smiles at him, gently pats his shoulder at the end of a night's work, and tells him to keep up the good work; he leaves the rehearsal taller.

His commitment is total. His character, Martini, is his and his alone. He begins to practise with other characters, with people he sees on TV or on the street, enjoying the release of jumping in behind their eyes, revelling in leaving his own troubled heart behind.

Once he spent hours as Errol Flynn, raking and swash-buckling his way across the kitchen, stabbing the mound of butter his mother had left out for tea. He even dived on to a mound of dirty clothes believing he was Captain Blood fighting a rising tide, flailing to save his life. His mother had watched him for a few moments, then shouted at him to behave.

'I'm Errol Flynn,' he had protested.

'I don't care if you're the Pope. Behave,' she had replied.

One morning he decides to spring a surprise on Sully. He waits until his mother is out of the room and just the two of them are left.

'What the hell is wrong with you?' Sully asks.

'Nuttin'.'

'Nuttin'? What's "nuttin'" when it's at home?' Sully is standing in front of him, towering above him, at the edge of the kitchen table, cramming a piece of toast into his mouth. 'You seem different.'

'Hey . . . I'm fine.'

'"Hey"? "Hey"? What the sweet Jesus is that? Are you coming down with something?'

'You wouldn't understand.'

'Try me, sunshine . . .'

James takes a deep breath. He lets the pause hang in the air, picks up a fork, studies it carefully, just like he had seen in the film the night before. He licks his lips, then says quietly, but with all the authority he can muster, 'I'm Al Pacino.'

'What?'

'I'm being Al Pacino.'

'You're being a friggin' pain, that's what you're being.'

'I knew you wouldn't understand.'

'Who in the sweet Nora is Al Pacino?'

'The guy in the film, the gangster. Forget it.'

'Oh, the guy in the Mafia. Right, I'm with you. In that *Godfather* drivel. Sure the country's full of fucking gangsters, you gobshite.'

'Leave me alone.'

'Is that why you're sitting there looking as if you just swallowed a lemon? This family's fucking cracked! It's not Al Pacino you need, it's a good dose of salts. Al fucking Pacino.'

James looks up from the table, places his hands palm upwards in his lap and stares at his foe, his head nodding on his shoulders.

'Hold on there, soldier. Now I'm quaking in my fucking boots.'

'Sully, language.'

James's mother bustles into the kitchen, her face flushed from lifting the bundle of clothes off the line, her hair sprayed across her face.

'Excuse me, Ann, but may I introduce Mr Al Pacino?'

'Who's he when he's at home?'

'Him.'

'Stop messing, Sully – I've an axe of a headache.'

'Your adored son thinks he's Al effin' Pacino, the gangster.'

'What's he on about, son?'

'Nuttin'.'

'See?' Sully shouts it, pointing a finger triumphantly at James.

'Sully, calm down – you're as big a child as he is.' She leans down into James's face and says quietly, 'He doesn't half get carried away, doesn't he?'

Death Al Pacino-style

Loyalty. I expect nothing less from my consigliere. *I liked the way she backed me up, took my side. That's the way it should be. He's a no-good nuttin' and soon he will die. He thinks he's running us into the town, so my* consigliere *can do her shopping and I can go to my gangster school. That's what he thinks. The truth is different. He will walk us to the van, and I will take my place calmly in the back.*

He's had it coming. This one I will take care of personally. I will take great pleasure in it. He will start the van, the consigliere *will behave as normal – she will fuss and tut about making sure she has everything with her – and I will wait patiently in the back, the clothes-line flex in my hands. My heart will be calm and steady because I am Al Pacino.*

As he leans forward to put the van into gear I will throw the flex round his neck and pull, using my knees to clamp hard on the back of his seat. I will see his face in the rear-view mirror bouncing in and out like a big fat purple ball. I will pull and pull and pull, and he will buck like da bull, and my consigliere *will sit on his hands so he can't use them.*

His tongue will hang down like a long loop and he will die, and I will calmly put away my flex and adjust my tie in the mirror, because I am Al Pacino.

10. The Grand Inquisitor

'Acting now, are we, son?'

'Er . . . yes, Father.'

'A whore's profession, son . . . Then again, if it keeps you off the streets . . .'

'Yes, Father.'

Father Leneghan is doing his rounds, standing painfully close to each boy he meets in the long corridor of the science block.

'Mr Shannon tells me you're inventive.'

'Does he, Father?'

'Now, if only you applied that to your studies, what a world it would be, eh?'

'Yes, Father.'

'Tell me, son, have we . . . ?'

'Yes, Father.'

'Had a little chat . . . ever?'

'Yes, Father.'

He watches as the priest ambles away, stopping to stand achingly close to another young boy, pushing his face into theirs. When no one is looking James gives the priest the finger.

Father Leneghan is the school principal, a pallid-skinned man in his mid-fifties. He punctuates everything he says with the flapping emphasis of his hands. That, coupled with two large ears that protrude from the sides of his head, has earned him the nickname 'Flappy'. He also has the habit of sitting silently and eyeing a boy for what seems like minutes on end, watching as he squirms in the leather chair across the desk from him in his office. James has often heard rumours of students sitting there nervously, sweat falling from their faces as Leneghan's pale eyes explore the pert fear on their bodies. He has heard that sometimes Leneghan gets up and walks round the heavy desk to the boy's side and stands by him, his hands buried in his trouser pockets, his knuckles protruding like black slugs through the cloth. He has been told that he stands that way for an age, his large flappy head inclined.

'Have you been a good boy?'

'Yes, Father.'

'No . . . You know what I mean, son.'

'I'm sorry, Father.'

'Sorry for what, son?'

'I don't know what you mean.'

They had been right. Father Leneghan had finally caught up with him one day, months before, as he had walked the same science corridor. He had appeared as if out of nowhere, moving into the centre of James's line of vision like a large black crow.

He had been led to Leneghan's office, had followed him up the back staircases of the school until they had reached a small dark room at the top of the building. First Leneghan had asked him if he was happy at the school and what were his favourite subjects, walking all over James's mumbled answers, impatiently waving his big soft fists. Then he made a note in his black notebook, closed it, leaned back in his chair and settled into the charged silence that James had so often heard about.

James had sat, perched uneasily in the leather armchair, for what seemed like an age. Father Leneghan's eyes seemed to glaze, as if a film of Cellophane had suddenly been placed in front of them. His lips were slightly parted, the yellowed enamel of his teeth showing.

Then Leneghan had risen slowly to his feet, rocked on his heels then crept over to the side of James's chair. James could hear the snorted breaths of the priest as they hit the back of his neck. Resolutely, almost desperately, he had stared ahead, eyelids lowered. Out of the corner of his eye he could glimpse the black outline of the priest's fingers through his trousers. They seemed to be moving, wriggling towards the centre of his groin.

'I mean, son, have you had any impure thoughts?'

'Impure thoughts, Father?'

'Yes, my son.'

'I don't know what you mean, Father.'

'I mean masturbation. My boy . . . do you masturbate?'

James had thought immediately of his hands beneath his bedcovers at night, of his fingers across his crotch. His jaw clenched. A new, darker hand now joined his beneath the covers, laying itself like a bristling tarantula across his lower abdomen. He knew that the priest now occupied his dreams, and with his laboured breaths and his flesh-obsessed hands he was there to stay.

He remembers mumbling denials as Father Leneghan had stood over him. He remembers the priest repeating the question, his hands buried forearm deep in his pockets, his wide, shovel face rich with perspiration.

'Do you masturbate?'

'Er . . . I . . . Not really, Father.'

After a few moments he glanced up towards the priest, angling his face so that he could grab a look at him. Father Leneghan's head was resting back on his large neck, and James found himself looking straight up the hairy cannons of the priest's nostrils. His eyes were closed, and

96

one large mug-like ear seemed to be shivering with expectation. He had looked transported, possessed. Suddenly the priest's lips had parted: his long slimy tongue had slid out and come to rest on his bottom lip.

Eventually Father Leneghan had moved back to his chair on the other side of the desk and dismissed him, his back to James, looking out of the window of his office. For a brief moment he had stood at the oak door of the priest's office, unsure whether to leave without saying something. Sensing this, the priest had growled that he should go. James can remember looking at the large, winged head, the balding spot at the back, and the large batlike ears that seemed to vibrate as the light had hit them.

Death at the Hands of the Inquisition

They have me on the rack. I can see the large flappy-eared head of Father Santiago Leneghan Lopez, the Grand Inquisitor, as it moves up and down my body, his nose sniffing and probing.

'There's sex on this man,' he says.

His large fleshy head stops for a moment above my genitals. I can hear his horse's breath snorting and sniffing.

'*Definitely slimy ungodly sex. Who have you been defiling, young man? Yourself? Others? Beasts?*'

I can see his large, winged ears dipping and vibrating as he pushes his face along my naked body.

'*Sex . . . Sex . . . Filthy sex . . . Tighten the screws, Father Sullivano.*'

I watch, my body contorting in torment, as Father Luke Sullivano turns the screws on the rack. The sinews of my body twang like the strings on a guitar. '*Confess! Confess to the Lord! Sex . . . sex . . . I can smell it. It rises like filth.*' *He lifts his head and sniffs. I can see up the two hairy barrels of his nostrils and nausea runs along my gut.* '*Bring me the sex tarantulas.*' *I see an ugly smile wiggle across his fat, slug-like lips.* '*They'll tell a tale, my boy, they'll tell a tale . . .*'

Father Sullivano returns with a small ebony box and hands it to the Grand Inquisitor, who caresses it as if it were a crystal ball. He places it across my belly button and opens a small hatch at the front of the box. He laughs, a thick taunting laugh. '*Go, my lovelies. Seek out the sex juices.*'

I strain my head upwards in terror and see two furry spiders creep through the hatch and on to the soft down of my belly.

'*If they bite you, my son, it is because they have picked up the scent of spilled seed. Death will be quick . . . and certain . . .*'

I feel them hunt along my body, foraging like large black hands. I see the vengeful glee on Father Sullivano's face as he shoos and encourages the spiders to do their work. As they sink their fangs into me I see Father Leneghan Lopez's head rock back on his shoulders and his eyes film over with a sordid ecstasy. As I die I hear him tell God to reject me.

11. *The Fury of His Other Face*

Early one evening the Ulster Griddle, the café where his mother works, rings, and James, fresh in from school and breathless from sprinting the final yards, answers the phone. There is a pause at the other end of the line, and James can hear the clink and rattle of plates.

'James?'

'Yes?'

'This is Marion McCartan. Are you OK?'

'Yes.'

'You sound got at, son.'

'No, I was running.'

'Oh, OK. Is your mammy there?'

'Hold on.'

James places the receiver down and goes to the living room. He sees his mother curled up on the settee, a blanket twisted round her body, a half-empty bottle of Gordon's Dry Gin on the coffee-table beside her.

'Marion?'

'Yes?'

'Mammy hasn't been too well. She's asleep.'

There is a pause. He shifts from one leg to the other.

'Is she drinking, James?'

He doesn't reply.

'Sully caused a scene at work today.'

'What?'

'He came in and started ranting. I think he had drink on him.'

'Ranting?'

'Yeah . . . about . . . Is she there, James?'

'She's asleep.'

'I told her she'd be better off without that lunatic.'

'What'd he do?'

'Oh, some nonsense about the dead staying dead – I dunno. He was tanked. The boss, Loughran, had to kick him out. It was embarrassing for your poor mammy. Well, tell her that I'll be round this evening after work, OK?'

'OK.' He hears the abrupt click of Marion's phone as she hangs up. He returns to the living room.

His mother is now lying on her back: her eyes are

open and still scented with sleep. She looks at him. 'Was that Marion?'

'Yes.'

'Is she coming round?'

He shrugs. His mother averts her eyes, and for a moment they stay that way.

'What did you tell her?'

'That you hadn't been too well.'

'She's not stupid. She's bloody nosy, but not stupid.'

She draws her knees up to her chest, her hands laced round her shins; her hair is gummed with sweat, her face smaller. She looks back at him.

'Mum . . .'

'What?'

'She told me.'

'Told you what, son?'

'About Sully . . . About today.'

'The stupid cow.'

'What happened?'

'Nothing.'

'Something happened. I'm not thick.'

'James, I have a headache that would cut steel. Now drop it.' She swings herself from the sofa, her feet landing in a misjudged thud on the carpet, her head flopping lazily over her knees. He goes to the kitchen and half fills the kettle, pulls a large mug down from the cupboard along with the jar of instant coffee and the damp bag of sugar. He can hear his mother shuffling into life next door. 'Make it strong, do you hear?'

He hears the creak of the stairs as she goes up, the thump of her steps as she clears the landing, the squeak of the bathroom taps and the roar of the water as it fills the bath. He looks out of the kitchen window and sees his reflection, the outline of his face held suspended in the glass. For a moment he stands and looks at the ghost of himself, then looks away, a tremor working its way across his hands.

Dishes are piled in the sink, veined with long blue-green seams of washing-up liquid. A loaf of bread lies on the scullery table, its slices lying across its surface like a discarded pack of cards. His mother's shoes lie at the foot of the table. Crumbs dot it and the floor, and loops of bacon rind lie on the draining-board. The fluorescent lightbulb overhead blinks, then catches, holding everything for a moment in a strange frieze, then begins to wink once more.

The glass fogs with the steam from the boiling kettle, misting and obscuring his reflection. He empties a table-spoonful of coffee into the mug and heaps a few mounds of sugar on top, then pours in the hot water and adds a little cold from the tap. He stirs it briskly and places it on the kitchen table. Then he goes to the cupboard above the fridge and pulls out a small wooden tray. He finds a packet of Anadin, pulls a sheet of tablets from the box, pops three from the bubbled foil, then places them by the mug of coffee.

Wearing her maple-patterned bathrobe, her wet hair held by a whipped-ice-cream twist of towel, his mother enters the kitchen, her feet slapping briskly on the bare concrete floor. She reaches for the coffee and the tablets. 'Did you put cold water in this?' She holds out the mug to him. The boy nods. She brings the coffee to her mouth, closes her eyes and, after the first tentative sip, drains the mug, her eyes bobbling beneath the closed lids. 'Don't look at me like that, James.'

'Like what?'

'You know full well.'

'I don't want him here.'

'Excuse me?'

'I said I don't want him here. I hate him.'

'Whose house is this?'

'Marion told me what happened.'

'So?'

'He's a pig.'

'I've met worse.'

'I hate him.'

'James, I don't need this. Now, for the last time, drop it.'

James goes to the living room and throws back the curtains. They squeal on their runners almost as if the room is protesting at being woken from its slumber. He opens the windows, and feels the beginnings of the cold night air on his face.

The Bass beer ashtray is full of cigarette butts; some have rimmed crimson crescents from his mother's lipstick. The gin bottle is open: its cap lies on the carpet; its sharp scent permeates the room. A bottle of tonic stands beside it, and next to that a half-eaten bowl of cornflakes, with a dead fly floating in the milky soup.

He picks stray butts off the table and carpet and, balancing everything in his hands and in the crook of his elbows, takes the ashtray and bottles to the kitchen. A plastic bin-liner sits in the middle of the floor, and his mother is aggressively cleaning the sink and the draining-board. 'Throw all that in the bin there and spray the living room.'

He takes the Glade air freshener and does as she has told him. He thinks of his other face beyond the kitchen window; he thinks of its two lonely eyes staring back at him, accusing him. He imagines its skinny body circling the house, looking for a way in, for a way to get at him. He shudders, and throws a quick look at the living-room window, expecting to see his other self. Quickly he rearranges the cushions on the settee and hurries to the kitchen, not daring to look back.

His mother stands hunched over the sink, her shoulders bowed and quivering. He can't see her face for her hair. Her body moves in long, convulsive spasms. Her hand snatches at the tap between retches, flushing cold water along the swirl of bile and half-digested food. She stops and rests her head on the sink's rim, gulping back the dry heaves, her hand still clasping the tap as much for support as anything else. James walks towards her. She turns her head away from him; small sounds come from her mouth, tiny noises of self-pleading.

He leads her upstairs, her hand in his. He remakes her bed, punching the pillows into shape, sweeping his hands across the sheets. She lies down, her knees coming up to her chest, her fists grabbing the bedclothes and pulling them over her head.

'I fucking hate him.' He whispers it, spits it at her curled and knotted shape.

He goes downstairs and runs the water in the kitchen sink, pouring capfuls of Domestos into it until the smell of vomit has gone, then locks the back door and turns off the kitchen light.

He closes the windows in the living room, hands tugging quickly at the latches, eyes scouring the garden; he pulls the curtains, and hurries away from them. He snaps the latch on the front door, checks that it's locked, and goes upstairs to his room. He undresses and reaches for his torch, then climbs into bed. He waits. After a while he drifts towards sleep, his grip on the the torch loosening.

Killing the Soft Boy in Me

I can see his house. I know he has turned off all the lights because I'm coming for him, and that he is pretending to be asleep, but really what he's doing is shivering in the dark like a little girl. I look like him and in a way I am him, but harder, deadlier. My skin is leathery, my eyes are dark and angry, and it's time I took his place. It's time for the mealy-mouthed wimp to die and for me to take over the business of his life. I'm standing outside in the cold night air, watching the stars fizz and blink. I like the dark. You see, you can hide in the dark.

I've given him lots of opportunities to deal with the bastard Sully, and to stand up to his mother, but he's weak and frightened. I don't believe in anything, only myself, and I hate everything. He knows that, and he knows that I'm coming for him – he could sense me last night, as he was looking out of the window, as he was being a good little girl and clearing up.

You see, I am made from the stuff that that creep Sully is made from. I want to hurt everything, I want everything dead. I like the war that rages in this pathetic little country. I like the bloodshed, I like the pain. As long as there is murder, as long as there is hate, I am doing my job. I can't wait to step into little James's dreams and begin my work, to change him, to turn him into an engine of hate. I want everyone dead. I want the priests dead. I want my mother dead. I want my teachers dead, except maybe one. He can live. I want babies dead. I want love dead. I want beauty dead. But, most of all, I want that soft part of me dead, the part that lies sleeping in his bed, his little girly hands clasping his torch, his soft neck as white as a cloud. I'll begin there.

12. *Marion and the Aftermath*

The next morning he wakes to the faint sound of the radio coming from the kitchen. He sits up in his bed and swings his legs off the side. He gets up and pulls back the curtains. Big-limbed clouds cruise across the sky, and the grass is a damp dark green from rainfall during the night. He leans his elbows on the window-ledge, cupping his face in his hands, his nose almost touching the glass. His eyes follow the caterpillar tracks of rain that run down the pane. He dresses. In the bathroom he slaps himself awake with ice-cold water, stopping to close his eyes as the previous night's events return to him. When he opens them again his mother has joined him in the bathroom. Her hair is teased up, her face is scrubbed and her eyes are moist with remorse. As she puts her arms round him, he can feel a coldness steal through his bones. He feels her hand in the small of his back as it rubs little circles of comfort. She pulls back from him, her hand steering his chin up so that his eyes look into hers.

'All we have is each other.'

'Yeah.'

'Did Marion McCartan call round last night?'

'I don't know. I think so – I fell asleep.'

'Well, I'm going in today. I'll sort it all out with her.'

'What happened yesterday, Mum?'

'Don't worry yourself.'

'Marion said he tore at you in front of everyone.'

'Come on now – we've started the day well, let's not ruin it.'

After a moment, he sees her eyes soften, as if she has thought better of her abruptness.

'What else did she have to say for herself?'

'She asked me if you'd been drinking – remember I told you?'

'Yes . . . No, I remember that, James, I'm not senile. Did she say anything else apart from that?'

'No.' He stares at her.

She wipes her palm slowly across his forehead, then pushes his hair back; he can feel his fringe spike up as it rises against her hand.

'Things are going to be different from now on.' She says the words as if she is rehearsing them for a speech she has to deliver somewhere far off in the future. She looks deep into her son's eyes. 'Do you love your mammy?'

He nods.

'Good boy.'

He eats his cereal, sucking the last dregs of milk from the bowl, raising it to his lips, feeling the cool slip of the milk as it hits the back of his throat. His mother drinks from a mug of coffee that she cradles beneath her chin, her gaze fixed on her son. He feels as if he should say something or that he should wrap her in his arms and hold her quietly, that anything less would be a betrayal.

'Is something wrong?'

'No.'

'OK. Get your stuff – I'll run you to school.'

She drops him at the gates, holding him for a few moments before he leaves the car. He finds himself telling her not to worry, that everything will work out fine. He can feel the clutch of her fingertips as they dig into his shoulder-blades. He watches as she drives away, sees her peek up into the rear-view mirror and adjust her hair. He sits on the small wall by the gates, his satchel dangling between his knees, watching the traffic as it makes its way up the main Armagh road, throwing up smoke-signal exhaust fumes, the lorries whining angrily as they rack down the gears.

He thinks of Marion McCartan's phone call the night before, and of the silences between their words. Marion is a Protestant but 'not so's you'd notice', as she is fond of saying. She is also his mother's closest friend but less so since Sully arrived on the scene. He can remember the countless evenings that Marion and his mother used to spend together, sitting on the worn sofa in their house, their stockinged legs crooked up beneath their buttocks. For hours they would sit that way, cigarettes passed between them, their friendship so deep that it was diffi-cult to tell them apart.

At first he had resented her. She had struck him as bloodless and cold. He would hide in his room, some-times skulking down to the kitchen to get a cold drink or a biscuit, grimacing at their whispered gossip, hating their loud laughter. Then he began to peer into the living room, through the crack in the kitchen door, and watch as Marion's skirt rode up her thighs. He would squat there twisting his neck to peek at the dark cloister that lay between her legs. One or twice he would get a quick rabbit-tail flash of her knickers as she uncrossed her legs and his mouth would dry. Then he would go back to bed, carrying with him the image of that knicker triangle and offer it to his dreams.

He can't help feeling that Marion holds a grudge for the way the friendship with his mother ended. When Sully had arrived his mother had dived head first into the dreams he had offered her, leaving all those around her staring dumbfounded from the shoreline of their lives, wondering where she had gone. James can remember fielding countless calls, explaining that his mother had gone out for the evening, the day or sometimes the week. He can remember one night in particular Marion shouting down the line that unless she got her act together his mother would soon be jobless as she couldn't cover for her much longer.

Sully detests Marion. He calls her an 'in-betweeny', neither a Taig nor a Prod, and that she should never have tried to be something she is not. Marion doesn't care much for him either, and James can remember when his mother and Marion had stood toe to toe and said things to one another that had brought spit and hate to their lips.

'Drinking's pulping your friggin' brain,' Marion had said.

'Shut your beak. You're only jealous.'

'Of that? Of that? I wouldn't scrape the bastard off my shoes if I stepped on him.'

'Get out,' his mother had said, advancing slowly on her friend, fists clenched.

He can remember the dramatic turn Marion made on the linoleum, reaching angrily for the door handle and shouting, 'He's a loser! He's a frigging loser!'

That was the last time she had been in their house as a friend. She sometimes calls in after work, but James knows it is different. When Sully had heard what had happened he had nodded self-importantly, his eyes widening slightly. 'She should have stuck to her own and not try to be what she's not.'

James had been sorry to see her go. By then he was fond of her, and he missed the inching upwards of that dress's hem.

A school bus pulls into the gates, swinging wide to make the turn, the driver using the ball of his hand to work the steering-wheel, his eyes fixed ahead, a cigarette dangling from his lips.

He stands, shouldering his satchel, and begins to walk the short distance to the town. He can feel the hungry gape of the school gateway on his back as he walks away. He jogs, pushing the air through his lungs. He thinks of the man in the alleyway. Had he imagined him? Maybe Sully was right: maybe he is a bit touched, maybe he is mad. As his feet thump the pavement he tries to forget him, to push the man and the firefly away, to pretend that he had never felt them, that he had never seen that beat of light flit by him on the day of the bomb. He is sprinting now, bending his body into his run. He thinks of the dream he had the night before when he had killed a part of himself, the part of him that looked to the ghost in things. Yes, maybe Sully and his mother were right: maybe he is the cause of all her pain. Yes, maybe he is the ghost.

Letter from a Firefly

Space
Far from Earth
High above Everything

Son,
It is cold. Cold since you questioned my existence. Warmth has seeped from me. I heard you as you ran into town the other day – your thoughts rose to reach me here high in space. It is the love of our friends and family that keeps us burning, that gives us heat, and yours is the only love I can count on. So the other day when you wondered, for the first time, if I was real, the light went out in me. Put your hand on your heart and say truthfully that you no longer believe I am with you. I guarantee that beneath your fingers as they lie across your heart you will feel not only your own heartbeat but another softer beat, as soft as a small bird's wings.

That's me. That has always been me. It has been a blessing to have a son such as you, someone to keep the flame of me alive, so you can imagine my shock when I heard you wish it otherwise the other day.

In your last 'thought' letter you asked me where souls go when they die. You have to understand there are certain things I can't tell you – it is forbidden – but it is a better place. That's all I can tell you. You also asked me if we had days and nights. There are no such things, no days, no nights, no hours, no minutes. And, no, I don't think badly of your mother. Now Sully, on the other hand, that's a different ball game. If I had such a thing as fists I would use them, no question. I was there the other day when he tore at your mother in the café. It wasn't pretty. Look after her. New fireflies join us all the time; there were a few on the day of that bomb. They are very shocked at first but they soon settle down. One woman kept saying she had to put her husband's tea on. We tried to tell her gently that the time for tea was over.

Anyway, it's time to go. Don't doubt me. Love your mother. Oh, by the way, I sometimes see your deaths when you perform them, or even think them. They are very true to life, or death, I should say. Love and continued warmth, I hope,

Your loving firefly father

116

13. The Invitation

At the end of the third week of rehearsals, Kerry decided to throw a party. She lives in a small farmhouse half-way between Newry and Crossmaglen, and arrives one day armed with her invitations. They show an unflattering portrait of Mr Shannon in a 1920s bathing-suit astride a hastily drawn road map. As Shannon tries to gain some order in the rehearsal room, she slips the invitations into people's hands and watches as they snigger. When one arrives with James, he glances at it, then tries to pass it back, but Cathal Murphy, sitting to his right, refuses to accept it, folding his arms and smirking at him.

Shannon is trying to place people into groups for the scene where his character, McMurphy, tries to get the television turned on so the inmates can watch a ball

117

game. He fusses around the rehearsal space, putting his hands on people's shoulders, pushing them into the position he requires, his moccasins slapping about on the concrete floor. One by one he calls on the people sitting around to join the action, yelling out their characters' names.

The small trestle table that serves as the nurses' station now has a crescent of people in front of it. James's name is called in a loud roar and he scurries up, shoving the invitation into his jeans pocket, trying desperately to keep a straight face. He is positioned at the front of the first group beside Patricia. Chin Chin, who is playing Chief Bowden, is placed at the back so that he looks like a lighthouse towering above the rocky peninsula of heads in front of him.

Suddenly Shannon stops. He looks like a hunting dog that has suddenly seen its prey. Slowly he bends down to retrieve one of the invitations that has fallen to the ground. He brings it up and looks at it, holding it by its corner as if it is infected. The room explodes with laughter. The actors' positioning, which Shannon has spent ages putting in place, dissolves. People are slapping each other on the back; some burst into applause. Kerry stands, right hand waving regally, her lips parted at the sweet glory of it all.

'I see we have a heartless cow in our midst.'

James watches as Shannon looks at the piece of paper

in his hand, then around at everyone's faces, a big grin sitting on his lips.

'Given the exactitude of the work that has obviously been poured on to this slip of paper, I trust Saturday evening will be the far side of mediocre, Miss Boyd.'

'You can bet on it, baby.'

That night as they sit down for dinner, James asks his mother if he can stay with his friend Plug on Saturday night as there is some work they need to do for a history exam.

'What exam?'

'History, the Versailles peace treaty.'

'The what?'

'The Versailles treaty, the First World War.'

She nods, her mouth full of chips. She doesn't say anything but continues eating.

It was a lie. He knows in his heart that his mother will forbid him to go to the party if she knows the truth. He had realised after their exchange in the kitchen, weeks before, that she didn't trust the whole idea of the play, most especially Mr Shannon whom, he now knows, she sees as a threat. In the time since their row, when she had caught him reading the play, and after what she had said in bed that night, he knows she tolerates his association with the man, but no more than that. He wonders what has made her so distrusting, so quick to judge.

Eventually, after a few moments of silent eating, she consents. He nods his thanks between mouthfuls of fried egg.

'I want you back here first thing on Sunday morning.'

'Yes, Mum.'

'First thing, do you hear?'

'Yes, Mum.'

Later that day he works on Plug, putting his plan to him, suggesting that he stay with him on the upcoming Saturday and that they can go to the party together. They are squeezed into the boys' locker rooms, just after lunch. A fight had been called at the eleven o'clock break that morning, boys eagerly whispering the news to one another on their way to a grabbed smoke or a hurried game of handball.

'Saturday night?'

'Yeah, Saturday night.'

'They're all poofs. I'll need iron underpants.'

'Don't flatter yourself, Plug.'

'I'm getting worried about you, Lavery. You'll be wearing pink cravats next.'

'Yeah, yeah, yeah. So?'

'What if I say no? You'll be in the deep muck then.'

'Shit – the expression is "deep shit". Come on – it's near Culloville.'

'Comanche country . . . I dunno . . . I'll need more than iron underpants up there.'

The fight is between two large boys only a year older than Plug and James, but nearer men than boys. They are due to leave school at the beginning of the following summer. They are muscular and fearless, and their rivalry is notorious. A small crescent of space has been cleared in the centre of the locker room, and all around boys cram into it, their eyes glittering. Seamus Byrne, the larger of the two boys, is the first to enter. The second, Clive Henessey, then takes his place in the small space. Both look as if they have just stepped out of a shower, or like two racehorses that have just run a very tight race.

'What brought this on today of all days?' Plug says, his voice a tiny girlish whisper of fright.

'I dunno. You're such a fucking professor, Plug.'

'I'm only wondering.'

'What about the party?'

'Someone's about to die and you're still on about the effin' party?'

For a moment the two fighters eye each other, an insolent smile playing across their lips, then rush forward, snagging themselves on each other's arms and legs, parting to get their breath. The first engagement has been so sharp, so swift that James almost missed it. A noise rings in the air, like the high-pitched squeal of trapped rabbits. The smaller boy has been cut. His lip is split like a busted cherry, and blood runs down his chin in a red line. He gives it a wipe and edges forward once more. This time they stay locked together for longer, their fists grabbing lumps of each other's hair, rocking together in a grotesque lullaby of pain.

'Go on – fucking kill him!'

James's shout is so vehement that it startles Plug, causing him almost to lose his footing. For a moment James believes he sees the two fighters stop and look his way, and they are no longer Bryne and Henessey, but Sully and he, fighting tooth and nail for the love of one woman, fighting to the death and beyond.

'Go on, do him! Do him!'

He sees Sully take a blow to the head, and James yells insanely. He is Errol Flynn in *Captain Blood* cutting his opponent's smug smile off his face with deft throws of his cutlass. He is Jason shattering the bony hordes of skeletons that mean to deny him the Golden Fleece. He is Montgomery Clift smashing his fist into John Wayne's face in *Red River*.

'Kill him, kill him, kill him!'

He sees Sully's head crack as it hits the floor and he sees himself climb over his prone body, biting and punching, nailing his rage to the bigger man's chin. He feels every swipe of the smaller boy's fist, every grunt of his throat, every hefty thump.

'Kill the fucker!'

'I never thought you had it in you,' he hears Plug say.

Once the more nimble boy gets the other down, he won't let him up, but lies on him as if they are two spent lovers still woven into the pattern of each other's bodies. The high-pitched squealing falls away, and there's a hush as the watching boys wait for the final act. The larger boy is face downwards and it soon becomes apparent that they are mumbling to one another.

'I'm going to get a knife.'

'Oh, yeah?'

'I'm going to get a fucking knife and I'm going to fucking stab you.'

'You are? You're going to stab me, are you? Say you're sorry,' Henessey says.

'I'm going to get a knife and kill you and your fucking family, I swear to Christ. I have a fucking knife at home and I'm going to fucking use it on your family.'

No one sees Shannon arrive, until his large hands reach down, pull Henessey up from the floor and slam him against a locker door. He puts his face into the boy's so that their noses are almost touching. He doesn't say anything, just holds him there. The boys disperse, slouching towards the locker-room exit.

'Don't bloody move. None of you! Don't you dare bloody move! I said, stay where you are.'

Everyone freezes.

'There's enough of this out there,' he says.

James sees him move close to Seamus Bryne, the larger boy, who is now on his feet.

'There's too bloody much of this.' Shannon waves a big arm in the direction of the world beyond the walls of their school. 'Too bloody much.'

For a moment he stands there, his head dipped, his large belly rising and falling, and then he goes out, leaving the hard truth of what he has said in the air behind him like the lie of bare, honest earth after a storm has ripped through it.

'OK,' Plug says, as they shuffle out of the locker room.

'OK what?'

'You shall go to the ball.'

'What?'

'You can stay at mine.'

'Good stuff.'

'You're no poof, you're a frustrated psychopath.'

Errol Flynn and the Cutlass of Death

I am Errol Flynn and I am revered as the greatest swordsman this side of the Irish border. I have lost count of how many have died at the point of my trusty cutlass of death. It was given to me by my dear friend Count Plug as he lay on his deathbed. He had made the same mistake I have just made: he fought for a woman's love, and was mortally wounded. I have seen the cutlass work a whole army of English invaders, slicing them down, like ragweed in a summer field. For a country, yes, for honour, yes, for a man's good name, yes: for all these things the cutlass is invincible, magical, and bestows superhuman powers on the man who wields it.

'Use it only for the ways of man and honour, never for a woman, for then the cutlass will turn on you and cause your end . . .'

That was what Count Plug had said as he had taken his last breath, his weakened hands clasping mine to the cutlass's jewelled hilt. For the years following I had obeyed the unwritten law of the cutlass. Although there were times when, I must confess, I came close to killing for a woman's love. I resisted until now.

The cutlass has just turned on me and stabbed me through the heart and as I write this my life is failing. I defended a woman's honour, challenging the oaf Baron von Sullivan to a duel for abusing our beauteous Queen Ann. The fight was no more than a couple of minutes old and I had looked forward to cutting my opponent's sneery grin from his face, when my left arm (I am left-handed) had swung in the air and driven the cutlass through my own heart.

I am now on my knees, and my breath is failing. All around I hear the baying of the local townspeople as they watch me die. As my head hits the ground I see my opponent bend to lift the cutlass from my hand, a hungry gleam beginning in his eyes. I smile because in doing that he has sealed his own fate, and as I die I bring my smile with me to the fireflies that ring Heaven's gates.

14. The Party

Lights blaze from every window of Kerry's house. Plug and James stand in the driveway, looking at the squat bungalow. James watches as party guests flit by the windows. He looks at Plug and his friend whistles at him, his face breaking into a smile.

'Have you got your iron underpants?'

'And my asbestos willy warmer.'

They begin to walk towards the house, their feet crunching on the gravel of the driveway.

As they reach it the door is thrown open, revealing the human clutter of the hallway. Bodies seem to be sewn into the garish fabric of the velvet wallpaper. Women lean into tight huddles, and one or two couples lurk in the doorways to other rooms.

'It's an orgy,' James says.

'It's Christmas,' Plug answers.

Suddenly Cathal Murphy appears; both boys' eyes immediately spot the pink polka-dot cravat he is wearing.

'Oh, no,' Plug whispers, and turns to bolt down the driveway. James grabs him by the elbow.

'Boys, lovely boys . . .'

'Cathal, this is my friend Plug.'

'What a name!'

'Yeah, it's short for Paul,' Plug says, his eyes lighting up with defiance.

'Really?'

'Yeah.'

'Well, you learn something new every day. And how are you, young James?'

'Good.'

'Splendid. Well, grab yourselves something to drink and to hell with the consequences, as they say. A pleasure to meet you, er . . . Plug.' He moves off down the hall, nodding and smiling at everyone he passes, his drink held aloft in his hand as if it were a trophy.

'What the effin' hell was that?'

'Plug!'

'Hey, big fella.'

James looks round to see Jarlath McAllister charging down the hall towards them, powering his way through the revellers. 'Jarlath.'

'How's she cuttin'?'

'Fine. Jarlath, this my friend . . . er . . .'

'How's it going?'

'All right,' Plug says.

'Any crack, literal or otherwise, eh?'

James blushes. Jarlath digs his shoulder playfully.

'We're on the lookout,' Plug says.

James gives his friend a look. Plug shrugs his shoulders and smirks at him.

'Good man, good man, that's the stuff. They don't come flockin' – know what I'm sayin'? – unless you're Val Doonican or Big Tom or someone like that. You have to hunt – know what I'm sayin'?'

'Yep,' Plug says, his head nodding seriously.

'Well, all the best, boys . . . And, big fella?'

'Yeah?'

'Take her handy . . .'

'Right. See you later.'

A man strides past the two boys and into the night air. It's a moment before James realises it's Chin Chin. He takes a few strides past them, then stops abruptly, swivelling on his Cuban heels to face them. He stares at the two boys as if he is peering through a dense fog,

'Lavery?'

'Chin Chin.'

Suddenly Chin Chin snaps his hand to his temple, his

fingers flattened in a salute. 'Maestro.' As he says the word, he inclines his head.

James returns the salute in a more relaxed fashion, as if he is a general at arms dismissing a trusty aide.

Chin Chin bows in Plug's direction, then turns and marches towards his car. When he reaches it, he stops for a second and turns back to the two boys. 'Shannon's been looking for you.'

He finds Shannon in Kerry's garden at the back of the house. Kerry leads him there, her chiffon dress billowing about her body, her sizeable breasts swathed in huge ruffs of cloth, a glass of punch gripped in her right hand. 'Did anyone ever tell you that you have the look of a young Laurence Harvey?'

'Er, no.'

'Well, you do . . . You do.' On the final coo of the word 'do' she gives him a long, lingering look, then runs her tongue along the upper rim of her lips. He can vaguely see the bulb-like silhouette of Shannon sitting on a garden bench. Before she goes Kerry thrusts her glass of punch into James's hand. 'Here, this'll keep you warm.'

He takes a seat beside his teacher, the smell of the punch rising to his nostrils, causing him to squint.

'Are you okay?' Shannon says.

'Yes.'

Silently they watch Kerry walk back up the garden,

her chiffon dress billowing about her body like a loosened cargo of ghosts.

They lapse into silence. It is this, the quieter man, whom James is most attracted to. The man who now sits beside him, an empty peace hanging over him like a half-remembered name. Suddenly Shannon's dainty hands make a light pan across his face, one after the other as if he is a large squirrel welcoming warmer months. He looks at James and stares at him for a moment.

'How goes it, fair Lavery?'

'Fine, sir.'

'Good . . . good.'

'Yes, sir.'

'What a sodding country . . .'

'Sir?'

'There is something rotten in the state of the Six Counties, Lavery.'

'Yes, sir.'

'"Now is the very witching time of night, when churchyards yawn, and hell itself breathes out contagion to this world" . . . Play?'

'*Hamlet*, sir.'

'It's all *Hamlet*, Lavery. Everything is fecking *Hamlet*.'

A tentative silence falls once more but, sensing it, Shannon rises quickly to his feet. 'Up and at 'em, Lavery, up and at 'em.'

'Yes, sir. Up and at 'em.'

'That's the stuff, young Lavery.'

As they begin to walk back towards the house, James suddenly remembers the glass of punch that Kerry had given him, and runs back to get it. He raises it quickly to his lips. As the liquid hits his tongue, he wonders briefly at the rush of warmth that rears deep in the seat of his soul.

Within the hour he is cajoled into performing one of his deaths. At first he resists, holding out his hands in front of him as if he is King Canute trying to force back a pressing tide. He is standing in Kerry's living room, people hemming him in on every side.

'Go on, you big girl's jersey. Jarlath's just sung "The Four Green Fields",' he hears Cathal Murphy whisper.

'Everyone does a turn – that's the law, baby,' Kerry shouts, as she passes with a breakfast tray laden with drinks. 'You next, my boy,' she says to Plug, as she wafts by him.

'I can't,' James says.

'Can,' Shannon says unhelpfully.

'I think it's bloody weird,' Patricia O'Hare says, her lipstick smudged and smeared so that she looks as if she has a clown's mouth.

'What is?' Cathal asks her.

'This death thing. It's weird,' she blurts.

'Oh, it's only a bit of fun.'

'Well, I don't think it's funny. It's bloody weird.'

'What's it to be, fair Lavery?' Shannon shouts, raising his glass in a toast.

'Hemlock, sir.'

'Ah, King Hamlet.'

'Yes, sir.'

'Fast, Lavery, you are fast – I can't for the life of me work out whether you are a genius or a charlatan, Lavery.'

'The latter, sir.'

Hemlock in My Ear

I love my garden. I love the peacefulness of it. I especially like it after a fall of rain when everything shines as if it has just been painted. I like nothing more than to lie here as I am doing now, in the late afternoon, and listen to the heavy hum of bees and watch flower petals float to the ground. I used to play with my son James here when he was younger. I used to chase him and tease him. Now, though, he is older and I am preparing him to take over the kingship of these Six Counties. He is a good boy, a little too sensitive for my liking but he means well.

I love the smell of the garden. I love the beauty. I often dream I am flying and the garden is holding me as if I am on a magic carpet. I think that I am a good king. I've always tried to be fair, to be good. I have a wife, Queen Ann, who is younger than I, and I worry about her sometimes. I think she thinks that the world is only here for her pleasure, and that saddens me. It makes her selfish. I also have a brother, Prince Sully, but we have never got on, I find him oafish, aggressive, and very jealous of me.

I have been having the strangest dreams recently. I dreamed that I had a problem with my right ear. It felt as if an earwig had crawled into it or some such thing and caused me great pain. In my dream Prince Sully and my queen are both peering into it – my ear, that is – and telling me that they can find nothing untoward. Then I go into horrible spasms and my garden lifts me up and carries me away, just as it has in many dreams many times before. And as I leave I see my brother and my queen below me kissing passionately on the hard earth where the garden used to be . . .

15. Kerry and the Fox

Hands explore him. He can feel the scramble of fingers across his skin and the sweep of a palm moving towards his groin. He blinks furiously, trying to remember. Lips meet his, thin, desperate lips nipping and digging. He feels a tongue against his. He feels sick. He tries to lift his head, but fails. He feels the hand break into the hairy part of his body. Disgust swirls in his gut. He arches his torso. He hears words of comfort come from the body that straddles his. He smells the odour of underarm and booze.

The kissing stops. His eyes become more accustomed to the dark. He can make out the tousle of the person's hair, the limp dangle of her bra strap and the white spill of her breast. Slowly he sees Kerry's face begin to take shape in front of him.

He can smell her sex. It frightens him. It smells like charcoal cinders in the rain. He watches as she pulls at his clothing, riding it up over his nipples, her hands flashing like daggers in the darkness. He hears her say, 'Sweet.' He puts his arms across his torso, and gingerly lifts his head. He hears the word 'please' leave his lips. Daylight is breaking. He can see a long tablet of light forming behind the curtains. He senses her lips descending to meet his again and tries to roll on to his side.

He remembers the glass moving towards his lips, and the sudden thrust of anticipation in his throat. He sees Shannon strut towards Kerry's back door. As he rolls across the bed, away from Kerry's desperate hands, pieces of the previous few hours fall into place. He can remember lying in the middle of the living-room floor shortly after the first drink. He remembers feeling the hemlock enter his ear and his body lock as it began to spasm. Everyone had laughed as he had sat bolt upright and begun to gag, his hands clutching the side of his head in pain. He remembers calling his queen's name.

Then he sees another glass placed before his lips; he sees the painted nails of the hand that holds it. This time the drink tastes harsher, and seems to scold the back of his throat. He can remember the slap of his vomit hitting the black soil of Kerry's garden and the stippled pattern it made on his plimsolls.

He is now lying on his side facing away from her, his arms crossed, holding himself. He feels her hot breath on his neck as she plants kisses there. Her hands are now moving across his back. He feels one reach his buttock. He jumps to his feet, head spinning. He fumbles with the fly of his jeans, cursing.

'What's the rush?' she says.

'Please . . .'

'Sssh . . . There's nothing to be afraid of, darling.'

The third drink had tasted of cough mixture. He was in Kerry's living room, and he remembers dropping the glass and hearing it smash what seemed like minutes later. Vaguely he recalls being led through a doorway into a small bedroom where coats hung, like the husks of bodies, from the corner of every cupboard and shelf. He remembers his body surrendering to the dense black power of the room.

He remembers Kerry's palm on his brow, the soothing breaths she blew across his face. He remembers her hand creeping across his belly before she left, leaving him staring unsteadily into the darkness.

He looks back at her. Her head is in her hands. 'Er . . . I'm going.'

'You sure, sweetheart?'

He nods. He can see her more clearly now: her face looks thuggish; her hair hangs heavy and lank about her shoulders. She looks manly, he thinks. Almost comically her left breast still hangs free of her dress, like a fleshy escarpment, its pointed nipple pert and bullet-like.

He fights his way clear of the room, stumbling against unfamiliar furniture. He hears her sigh. He doesn't look back but focuses on reaching the kitchen door. He wrenches it open and lurches through it, straight into a scrum of vomiting. Nothing comes, only small straggly threads of saliva. Eventually he stands up and walks in the direction of his home.

Once or twice he throws a look back towards the house and imagines her lying in her rumpled bed, her exposed breast spilling across her upper body. He wonders how he can face everyone at the next rehearsal. He imagines their faces, their gossipy nods and their smirks. He thinks about his friend Plug. He feels a stabbing of guilt in his heart.

He shakes his head, raises his hands to his face and looks up at the morning sky. Everything seems bled of colour, as if he is walking in an old newsreel. He thinks of his father and the photograph. He thinks of him sealed in its flat landscape, endlessly looking out at a world that didn't care. He thinks of the half-smile on his father's face, the soft smile of someone who loved all that life was showing him.

He shudders, as if someone has quickly passed by him and stolen a look at the workings of his heart. He stops and looks around him, at the hedgerows and the tops of the trees. Then he feels foolish, ashamed of the panic in his glances. He tells himself that the presence he feels is only his heart regarding itself.

He sees a fox break free of the shuck to his left, watches as it runs to the far line of grass where it stops suddenly and looks at him. For a moment their eyes lock. He envies the self-possessed gleam of its stare, the soft amber glow of wildness. He wonders what the fox sees when it looks at him. Did it feel sorrow for the two-footed beast that was caught at the threshold of two worlds?

By the time he has reached his home and crept stealthily to bed he has told himself that no one need know about Kerry. He will tell Plug he passed out in her spare room, woke later that night and walked home. He goes to bed and sinks into a heavy sleep, dreaming of falling into a dark room that spins on the point of one of its corners, in which he scrambles frantically to stand upright.

Then the dream changes. The spinning continues, but this time he is being spun in the deep cavern of Kerry's mouth, his thin, delicate body turning on the point of her tongue. Eventually he is spat out, like a torn morsel of food, and lies crumpled on the ground looking up at Kerry's giantess face and seeing with horror that she has the hunting eyes of a fox, in which desire beats with a soft amber glow.

In the Mouth of a Fox

I must pretend to be dead: that way I am safe. I can feel the large fox's presence. I must keep my eyes tightly closed and stop my small chest from moving up and down. My wing is broken. I caught it on a telegraph wire as I came down from the sky to grab a sip of water from the lake by the road. I don't know if I will ever fly again, but first things first: I must survive the next few moments. I think of my dear aunt Teezy, a fine fat swallow who has flown many miles, over many continents. I rely on my auntie Teezy: she looks after me. It was she who told me about my father, a very fine proud swallow, who had flown away years before.

Teezy always told me that the main thing about a fox is that it likes to play with its prey and watch as it struggles to get away. On the other hand, if it has recently eaten it will pass by a dead bird. Maybe it is nothing more than an old swallow's tale, but I will soon find out. I must stay still. I will pretend I am not here. I am just a marking on the road. I don't exist, I'm telling myself. I have no history, no father, no mother, not even an aunt Teezy.

It is smelling me, I can feel its wet nose rubbing against my tummy feathers, and I can hear its tongue licking and slurping. It hasn't eaten recently: it is going to eat me whole. I must get away. I struggle to my feet and, dragging my broken wing behind me, I try to flee. I know I look pathetic and ridiculous but, you see, my life depends on it.

I don't get very far before I feel the mouth of the fox enclose me and its tongue run across my body. It is warmer in here than I thought it would be. I feel myself being spun round and round like a little acorn in the wind. It is making me giddy and I catch glimpses of the outside world through the fox's teeth.

I am spat out, and now I lie on the ground all wet and soggy looking up at the big red face of the fox. It opens its jaws and this time I know it will not play with me but finish me off with one crunch of its large yellow teeth. As it bends its head towards me to kill me, I look deep into its eyes and know that they remind me of someone. Someone who flew away a long time ago.

16. The Post-mortem

The following Monday James misses rehearsal, preferring to sit in his bedroom locked in his thoughts, shaking
the shame from his mind as he remembers his encounter
with Kerry. The thought of her old hands on his skin
fills him with revulsion. For the whole evening he sits
and looks out of the window at the kingdoms of clouds
that reel and twist through the sky. He stares at the
spirals of mist and darkened sky, and wishes himself
there, being turned this way and that in the sweet flavour
of their air. He watches until it is dark, then waits until
the stars come out and tries to guess which one is his
father. After a while he gives up, closes the curtains, and
drifts off into a dark starless sleep.

At two thirty on Tuesday afternoon, on his way to

religious studies, Mr Shannon comes up to him. He stops
James by blocking his route, and by holding his briefcase level with his downward gaze so that James has no
choice but to read the embossed initials of the teacher's
name: A. G. S. Shannon.

'Remember me?'

He looks up into the fierce, playful gaze of the teacher's
eyes. 'Yes, sir.'

'Good, because for a moment I thought a new boy
had enrolled in this estimable seat of learning, one with
your questionable good looks but without the spirit. A
doppelgänger, in fact.'

'Yes, sir.'

'Where are you off to?'

'Religious studies, sir.'

'And with whom do you have that dubious pleasure?'

'Father Boyle, sir.'

By now the other boys have gone, the two-thirty bell
for class having cleared the corridors as if a plague has
been declared. One boy hurtles along the corridor
towards them.

'Don't run, McCracken. Walk with dignity at all times.'

McCracken slows to a stumbling walk, his legs almost
wobbling in protest, his school tie hanging undone about
his shoulders.

'Do up your tie, McCracken, you look . . . forlorn.'

He does up his tie and throws a quizzical look at

143

James, then disappears round the corner. Shannon looks at James and winks as they hear McCracken's feet quicken, then resume their sprint.

'Accompany me, Lavery.'

'Where to, sir?'

'The staff room.'

'But, sir –'

'Don't fret yourself about Boyle – forgive me, *Father* Boyle – I will take care of it. Now, let's boogie.'

They enter the staff room, which is deserted apart from Mr Hogben. He sits in the far corner of the room surrounded by exercise books, his hair, as usual, tufted and dishevelled.

'Mr Hogben.'

'Mr Shannon.'

Shannon slaps his briefcase down heavily on the large communal table that sits in the middle of the room. 'Do you want a cup of tea or coffee, Lavery?'

'Yes, sir.'

'Which?'

'Tea . . . sir.'

Hogben looks up and said, 'Two sugars, Master Lavery.'

'Sorry, sir.'

'I take two sugars in my tea – and milk. That's the boy.'

'Yes, sir.'

Once the tea is made and Hogben has taken delivery of his, James sits opposite Shannon at the far end of the room to Hogben, the two of them throwing Hogben occasional glances of impatience. 'Did you want one, sir?'

'What?'

'Tea or coffee, sir?'

'No . . . thank you, Lavery.'

He sips his tea, feeling uneasy in this teachers' den, the steam from his cup tickling the inside of his nose.

'Where were you last night?'

'I was at home, sir.'

'You were due at rehearsal, or had it escaped your notice?'

'No, sir.'

'No, sir, no, sir – what does that mean?'

'No, sir, it hadn't escaped my notice.'

'Where were you?'

'At home, sir.'

'Do I have to drag every tired response out of you, Lavery? The question I'm asking, in case you hadn't guessed, is why?'

'Why what, sir?'

'Is everything all right, Lavery?'

'What do you mean, sir?'

'At home. Is everything all right at home?'

At that moment Hogben stands and begins to gather his notebooks. Shannon waits. Before Hogben leaves he comes and stands by them, his hand fiddling with a few straggles of his renegade hair. 'Is he any good, then?' he asks.

'Who, Mr Hogben?'

'This reprobate.'

'He'll do, Mr Hogben, he'll do.'

'I couldn't bloody do it, I tell you – you know, act.'

'I know you couldn't, Mr Hogben,' Shannon says.

'I'll leave you to it, then, Mr Shannon.'

'Yes, Mr Hogben.'

And, with a final dipped shunt of his head, Hogben leaves. Shannon watches him go. 'What age are you, Lavery?'

'Just gone seventeen, sir.'

'Well, you have more than enough time to avoid a fate like that. How much did you have to drink the other night?'

Although he has been expecting some kind of postmortem on the events of the other night, the question still brings a sting of surprise to James's face. 'I don't know, sir.'

'Do you remember me asking you to stop?'

'No, sir.'

'Well, I did.'

'Sorry, sir.'

'Be careful, Lavery. Is that why you skipped rehearsals?'

'Kind of . . .'

'How is your mother?'

'Fine, sir . . . Why?'

'No reason, Lavery. Drink is a baleful enemy. Be careful.'

'Yes, sir.'

'Send your mother my best . . . And be vigilant, Lavery
. . . And be at the next rehearsal . . . come hell or high
water. Understood?'

'Sir.'

'Good man. Pow-wow over, Lavery.'

'Yes, sir.'

When he leaves the staff room his head is bowed in
thought. He feels that Shannon was saying something
about his mother, and about him, as if what she has is
contagious and that James has caught it. It unsettles him.
It makes him feel dirty, infected. He decides he will be
at the next rehearsal come what may, Kerry or no Kerry.
He is glad that Shannon hadn't mentioned her, and he
feels sure he has got away with it. All that remains is to
outface her, the manly woman, and her wide, hungry
arms.

'What's Your Poison?'

*She is holding out the chalice towards me. Her lips are
still moist from where she has drunk. I look at her: I*

know she is dying and that she wants to see me drink from the chalice before she goes. She can see that I am not sure. What am I to do? I love her but I don't want to go the same way as her, with bitter poison as my last taste of this world. Reluctantly I take the chalice and look at the blood-red liquid, at how it gleams and glistens against the inside of its walls.

'Drink,' she says, her voice failing, her eyes filming as Death comes to call. 'Drink . . . for me . . .'

'I can't,' I say.

'Yes, you can. We're going to join your father the king in Heaven tonight. Drink. Your queen commands you to drink.'

I look at her lying on her gilt-edged cushion, her lips slightly parted, her jewelled throat winking, and think that Egypt is about to lose the finest queen it has ever seen. Her faithful eunuch, Mephet Lucius Sullivano, stands to one side, fanning her with large ostrich feathers, his shaved head quivering with grief.

'Stop whingeing, Lucius!' she scolds. Then she turns her attention back to me, once more offering me the chalice. 'Your dead father, the immortal Pharaoh, commands it . . .'

This time her voice is angry and harsh. Reluctantly I raise the chalice to my lips and feel the bitter mixture rush into my mouth. I swallow and see a smile begin at the corners of her lips, and her arms reach out to enfold

148

me. I lay my head on her breast and wait for death to fall, smiling to myself because what is killing her is killing me too.

17. Logs

The next day after school he sees Sully's white van parked in their yard, its bald front tyres exposed in a wheel lock. He can hear Sully at the back of it, alternating between grunts and whistles. He's moving the logs. At last he's moving the logs. After weeks of complaints and snorts of impatience from the neighbours, Sully is moving the logs. What does he want? What is he after? Nothing comes free with someone like Sully. Suddenly Sully's face appears over one of the van doors, his face bordered by a fuzz of beard.

'Sully.'

'Well, don't just stand there being fucking enigmatic, give us a hand with these logs.'

James doesn't move. He stays where he is. Sully looks at him for a moment and says, 'Suit yourself.'

He watches as Sully's head disappears once more behind the van doors. He hears the thump of the logs hitting the back of the wood box and the squelch of Sully's wellingtons as he roots around in the shed. After three or four trips, Sully stops and marches over to James. 'Listen, kid.'

Here it comes. Here comes the 'cowboy talk', James thinks. He watches as Sully squints into the distance. For a moment he has to try to stop himself bursting into laughter.

'OK. Listen, kid,' he says, biting softly on his lower lip. 'Your mammy asked me to speak to you. We've . . . I've something to tell you, kid.'

'Yeah?'

'Yeah.'

'So?'

'Goddammit! I tell you, you don't make it easy on a guy, kid.'

How pathetic he seems, James thinks, with his 'goddam' gunfighter language. He turns to go into the house.

'Your mammy and me,' Sully says.

'What?' He turns back, the swivel of his body hard and fast, bringing a burp of surprise to Sully's lips.

'Er . . . we've decided to give it a real go, a proper lash of the whip.'

'What do you mean?'

'I'm moving in . . . you know, properly.'

For a moment James feels his body continuing, one

foot in front of the other until he has turned away, his face pointing towards the house.

'We've talked hard about it, kid, and we both think it makes a lot of sense. You know? All this coming and going, it's no good for man nor beast.'

'Fuck.' He says it quietly to himself, and to the listening light that he knows hovers out there in the black anchor of space.

'Listen, James, we never got off on the right foot so maybe this is a chance . . . You know . . . We can get to know each other. I think the world of your mammy . . . and you. And, listen, I know I'm not your father . . . but . . .'

James swivels back to face Sully. How dare you? his eyes say. How dare you speak the word?

Sully slowly walks closer to him. 'James, come on, kid. This is really stupid – I'm your friend.' Sully puts his hands gently on his shoulders. 'Come on, let's make a go of it, eh?'

He is almost afraid to lift his head and look at Sully directly, afraid of the softness he knows will lie in the man's eyes.

'You know all that stuff weeks back about the man you thought you saw, the light and all that stuff, it set your mammy back. It really upset her. It's time to move on . . . We all have to move on . . . Somewhere . . . Some time . . . We all have to move on . . .'

Slowly James lifts his head until his eyes are level with Sully's. His body feels as if it is on fire, at war with the air around it. 'I hate you.'

'No, you don't. You don't hate me. Come on, now, them's strong words. Strong fucking words, James. Hate's destroyed this place.'

'I do – I fucking hate you.'

He pulls himself free and runs for the front door. He tugs his satchel round to his front, opens its flap, his hands diving in to rummage for his house keys. As they clear the lip of the bag he loses his grip on them so that they arc over his head and land with a jangle somewhere on the road. He begins to kick the front door, aiming hard, brutal blows at it, feeling shivers of pain run up his shins.

'Hey! Hey! Jimmy, stop that! Come on, now, that's enough.'

Sully has reached him, and for a moment he flounders. The door heaves, bouncing back and forward on the Chubb lock as James's feet pound it. The rhythm is slower now, as his legs tire, his toes pulsing with daggers of pain. He feels as if he is kicking through water. Eventually he stops, head bowed, breath charging.

'Feel better?'

James doesn't reply but stands where he is. Sully retrieves the keys and unlocks the door, shoving it open, then pulls the keys out of the lock and fumbles to replace them in James's satchel, as if nothing has happened. They both stand for a moment in front of the open door: small splinters of wood lie on the threshold. The hall is dark and dense with silence; it seems to come out to meet them. Sully goes inside first and turns back, almost as if to nod that it is safe for James to follow. James watches as Sully turns at the end of the short hallway and hears the scuttle of his fingers on the wallpaper in the living room as they search for the light switch. When Sully reappears in the doorway he looks awkward and sheepish, and waits for a moment, then half-heartedly waves a hand. 'Come on.'

They stand by the fireplace, hearing the wind in the chimney breast. James picks at the strap of his satchel; Sully seems half poised to leave, one shoulder lifted as he tries to decide.

'Your mum should be home soon. Maybe I'll hang on for her.'

It sounded as if he was asking permission, but James ignores him.

'I'll go and finish stacking those logs.'

PS to a Firefly

11 Erin Grove
Carrickburren
Date: A bad day
Year: One of them

Father,
I'm lying here in my room. I'm holding the photo-
graph of you from when you had human form.
Everyone tells me that one day I will look exactly
like you. Teezy especially believes it. She used to say
it to me all the time, though not so much now. You
know, of course, why I'm contacting you. I'm sure I
could feel you the other day when that long streak
of piss told me his news. I was sure I could feel you
blink in disbelief, as if the light had gone out in you
for a second. She didn't even have the nerve to tell
me herself. She got him to do it with his John
Wayne fucking language. (Excuse my words. Is that
a mark against me?) He's not a patch on you – he
couldn't lace your boots (that is, if you had any).

I gave as good as I got, though. I let him know. I
let them both know. I only wish the door had been

his fat head. What am I going to do? His big, fat, greasy body is going to be squeezing into every corner of our house. I have to admit I've been crying. That's not very manly, is it? I hit myself around the side of the head to stop the tears, but after a while it hurt too much.

My heart is hard and quiet, and I have to admit I'm angry with you, I'm sorry but I am. It's all right for you, high above everything, welcoming other fireflies, like some kind of shiny RUC man. I know it's an important job, but what about me? What about your son? You've just left me here, with them, with their cooey love and their horrible fights. Maybe I should just look after myself and forget about you. I'm sorry, but the world is cold and no amount of light can warm it.

James

18. Amends

The next rehearsal is a muted affair. As usual Kerry arrives late. James dips his head when she enters, his hair falling helpfully across his eyes. He secretly peers at her as she thumps her body into its seat. He is relieved that she has sat far across the room from him and even more relieved that she seems intent on bending Chin Chin's ear.

'Good do the other night.'

James turns to see Jarlath McAllister's ruddy face peering into his. 'Yeah.'

'Fuck, there was some booze there. Not much talent, mind you.'

'No.'

'What time did you leave?'

'Er . . . late.'

157

'A few of us went on to Dundalk and drank the piece out there.'

'Right.'

'I didn't see you leave.'

'It was after – after you.'

'She can throw a great shindig, your woman. Fine handsome lump of a one she is too.'

'Yes.'

They both look over at Kerry.

'I wouldn't mind rummaging around in there of a windy evening . . . would you?'

He knows she has seen him – he can tell from the way her eyes periodically flicker in his direction. There is a stallion-like arrogance to the way she shakes her head, as if she is intent on sending him a message. In the harsh light of the rehearsal room, she looks older and more fragile, long worry lines skirting her full mouth like the fine, bloodless veins on a leaf. At one point Chin Chin reaches out and presses a large hand on to her knee. James thinks of the hard force of her touch in the pale morning light the week before, the needy tremor of her fingers on his belly and the loneliness in her eyes.

'Are you with us, Master Lavery?'

He looks up to see Shannon standing over him. 'Yes, sir.'

'Good man. Arm yourself. We are five minutes from running the play.'

'Yes, sir.'

'Sean. We're not at school now.'

It is a messy business. Entrances are missed, lines and props are dropped. At one point Kerry, as Nurse Ratchet, drops a whole tray of medication, shouting, 'Shit,' at the top of her voice. The play shudders to a halt as everyone bursts into laughter. Shannon, as McMurphy, covers every inch of the playing space, his stocky legs propelling him to and fro like a man whose house is on fire, one eye on his character, the other on the ragged attempts of his cast to coax the play into life.

Chin Chin, as Chief Bowden, moves as if every step has the ponderous weight of an oak tree behind it. James's heart isn't in it and the big black bird he had conjured on to his bedroom wall all those weeks before now seems indulgent and pointless. His head is numb, his thoughts jarred by the news Sully had given him the previous day, and his performance feels hard and angry.

Jarlath, as the shy Billy Bibbit, stutters so much at one point that Chin Chin quietly suggests they phone a doctor. Cathal Murphy, as Mr Henderson, seems to be the only one who brings any dignity to the proceedings. He is word perfect and views the chaos around him with the cool regard of a practised poker player.

When they finish, Shannon orders them to arrange their chairs in a semi-circle around him. His face is bathed in sweat and his large belly rises and falls as he regains his breath. 'We have ten days and ten nights before we open in Belfast for the amateur festival there, and time as we know waits for no man . . . or woman. What I have just witnessed would give "mediocre" a bad name.'

Kerry says something quietly to Patricia that causes her to laugh. For a moment Shannon stares at both of them, a faint gleam of paranoia growing in his eye. 'Kerry Boyd, know your props and your lines. Patricia Rooney, you are a staff nurse, not a psychopath.'

He turns his attention to the men, taking a deep breath before he continues. 'Chin Chin, he is not Boris Karloff, son of Frankenstein. He is a human being, which may be hard for you to grasp, but a feeling, caring human being none the less. Lavery, where were you? Well?'

'Here, sir.'

'Not by my reckoning, son. Try to keep your accent this side of the Adriatic Sea, Lavery. And, Jarlath, try and lose the "Culchie" twang and please, please, try to complete a sentence this side of Christmas. Your character has a stutter, not a terminal illness.'

'What about you?' Kerry asks.

'What about me?'

'Do we give you some criticism?'

'No, that's the director's remit.'

'But you're the director.'

'Exactly. So I will have a private chat with myself later.'

'That'll be a bit one-sided,' Chin Chin says.

As they leave the rehearsal room James catches Kerry's eye. She smiles at him, a tender, sorrowful smile. He smiles back and quickly looks away, embarrassed but grateful that some kind of amends have been made.

On his way home he dreams of love. The love he has read of in books, chivalrous, generous love, King Arthur love, the love of warriors and knights, the love that has the ear of God. He knows that it doesn't sit in Kerry's wide, desperate arms, in her needy, hungry eyes.

He passes a foot patrol on a deserted side-street – he can see the glow of their night torches as he approaches them, weaving red-eyed patterns in the dimly lit street. He bows his head as he passes them, his ears primed in case they order him to stop. They don't.

He thinks of his row with Sully the day before, and wonders when he will be moving in, with his oily layabout hands, fussing and bossing his mother around. He wonders how she can betray him, without so much as an excuse-me or a by-your-leave. He doesn't want their kind of love. They can keep it. Their selfish, pay-me-back, you-owe-me love. He thinks of the anger they bring to each other, the disappointment they both seem so ready to lay at one another's feet. That's not love. He finds himself saying it softly at first and then more forcefully: 'That's not love. No way!' He shouts it, his voice ringing off the walls of the street.

He throws a look behind him, and notes that the army

patrol has stopped and are pointing their red-eyed torches his way. He freezes as the little red tracks flit across his body, like little devil's eyes, squirming across his frigid body.

'Oi! Keep it down.'

The soldiers waft their torches off him and resume their snail-paced patrol.

When he loves it will be with the soft petals of longing, and he will lay them at his love's feet like a perfumed carpet. He will give his heart to the altar of her soul. Yes, he will know the true meaning of the word 'love'.

For Love

We haven't met yet, but I know you are there some-where, out there in the big world going about your life, and I am here in bed, my hands linked across my lower stomach. I often think of you and wonder if we will know each other when we meet. I am an only child and my mother's boyfriend is about to move in with us. She is all excited, and tonight when I came home from rehearsals I went into her room where she was sleeping. It smelt of old drink as usual and wet-cigarette breath. I stood by her bed, just like she had done with me so many times. I stood like a ghost who had nowhere to go and I watched the tiny tick of her pulse in her neck.

I asked her why she hadn't told me. I asked her if she hated me that much. 'Why?' I said. 'Why?'

A part of me wanted to put her big flowery pillow over her mouth, but I didn't, of course, and all I could think of was that soon Sully would be lying in that same bed and that it would be his, too, because he wouldn't be leaving when daybreak came.

Then I told her . . .

'That's not love,' I said. 'That's not love.'

The second time I shouted it, and for a moment I thought I had woken her, but she was in too much of a stupor.

Do you wonder about me too? One day we will meet. I collect deaths so I could die in many different ways for your love. I could take poison for you, or a knife, or I could be gunned down protecting you from rapists. I could go to the guillotine for you, or fight a duel like the knights did for their queen. It's late and my hands are moving lower. Even though we haven't met I will imagine they are your hands, even though I know I will be condemned for loving you. Then I will imagine that I am burning at a stake in hell but I won't mind because it will have been for you and the glory of your love.

19. D-Day

'Don't look at me like that – I've tried to talk to you and this is the thanks I get.'

'You haven't talked to me. You just told me.'

'Don't be stupid.'

'You always just tell me.'

'James, I'm in no mood for lip.'

'I'll stay with Teezy.'

'Stay where you like.'

It's the weekend. Saturday. One day until Sully's appointed moving-in. His mother roams about the kitchen like a caged bird. He watches as she lifts the kettle before placing it back in the exact spot it was in before. She does the same with the teapot and the sugar bowl.

'Listen, James, he thinks the world of you . . . of us both. Give him a chance.'

'No.'

When he slams the back door behind him, a part of him revels in its loud thump, and as he stomps his way to Teezy's house he curses the blue sky above him, he curses Sully, and wishes he were far away, far from the politics of his own life.

'Leave them to it, son. Rise above it.'

'Why?'

'It's just better that way. They've made their bed . . .'

'He's a selfish bastard.'

'James, no language in front of me.'

'But, Teezy, he hates me.'

'No one truly hates anyone, James. Try to remember that.'

'But, Teezy . . .'

'Listen, son, I know it's hard to fathom what people see in each other but let them get on with it.'

He watches as her heavy body fusses around him, now and then resting her hands on his shoulders, or the cool part of his neck.

'Now come on, eat. There's nothing on you.'

'I'm fine.'

'No, you're not. You've a face on you would scare God out of his throne.'

'Teezy . . .'

'You know and I know he's a loser. Now, do your auntie a favour and put up with it. Not for him, for your mammy. She's not up to this fighting and carrying on.'

'Why does everyone always go on about her? How she's this and she's that. What about me?'

'Listen, I'll make a deal with you. You behave yourself and I'll treat you to a fine holiday this summer. A fine lovely holiday where you can forget about all this nonsense. Deal?'

'That's ages off. He'll be all over the house. "This is mine, kid, and you better goddam believe it."'

She smiles as he does his impression of Sully, and for a moment he forgets his pain and smiles back. She sits down at the table beside him, reaches out, takes his hand and puts it in hers. He can feel the heavy warmth of her touch. He looks at her, at her big head and the soft love in her eyes.

'When I was your age everything was so important. Everything was life or death. It's not that way at all, son. Things are much slower than you think. And one way or another we all end up back where we began. We all end up waiting . . .'

'Did you never have a boyfriend, Teezy, or a . . . ?'

'What – a husband? Damn the fears, I've enough trouble keeping this old corpse of mine ticking over without having to look out for anyone else – especially not a man.'

'But you look out for me.'

'Ah, but you're different. You're special.'

'I don't feel special. I feel stupid and –'

'Stop right there, my boy, right there.' She raises one of her large hands in front of his face. Then she leans her face into his and says, 'If I say you're special it means you're special, because this is my house and I make the rules. OK?'

'OK.'

'Good. And if you must know there was someone once. He lived up by the Green Road. This is years ago before they put up those concrete boxes they have a nerve to call houses. He was a handsome lump of a man with big rosy cheeks. He always looked as if he'd just been sitting by a fire.'

'What was his name?'

'Fintan.'

'Fintan?'

'Fintan Walsh. A fine man he was.'

'And what happened?'

'Well, we were courting on and off for three years or so. His father owned that land up behind that new school there . . . What's it called?'

'St Peter's,' he says.

'That's right, St Peter's. Anyway . . .'

'Yeah?'

'Ah, it's a lifetime ago, son.'

167

'What happened, Teezy?'

'He broke it off. He said he had been promised to some girl. There was some arrangement made with some farmer owned a lock of land over by Meigh. It was different in those days, son. Different ways.'

'What? He married someone else?'

'After a while he did.'

'That's mad.'

'You see, son, we all have our crosses to bear. It just depends on the heaviness of the wood. Now, remember our deal and this summer you'll be like a pig in muck and you can forget about Sully and your mammy. Now, I'll sort it out with them. All you have to do is behave.'

She gets up slowly, puts her hands on her hips and regards him for a moment. Then, very softly, she says, 'I'll stick the kettle on so we can wet our beaks.'

The next evening he can hear them below in the scullery. Sully is in. He imagines them sitting in front of the fire, their glasses full. He sees his mother's face, her hair piled up in swirls, held by the pins he had passed to her patiently only hours before. She had been standing before the bathroom mirror, her lips elastically working in her lipstick. 'Midnight Cherry,' she had said.

He had watched her shade her eyes, watched them become bluer. He had watched her become her other self, the one who brought Sully the promises she thought he wanted. He sees her now, her black pencil skirt holding her taut, her body draped in Sully's direction, angled in offering, her mascara eyes, slow-lidded from the whisky he brought.

'To a new life,' he had announced, as he stood in the doorway, wearing his trademark lopsided grin, which said it all. Yes, he can see the two of them huddling and cuddling by the fire's warmth, his mother licking her Midnight Cherried lips.

Sully and his mother will sleep in the low room, in her bed, the bed that is no longer just hers. Yes, Sully is in. More dangerous than before, more grinning, more full of shit than he has ever been, because now he is the master of all he surveys.

Eventually James could stand it no longer and had left them to it, to their coded winks and lust-filled silences. He had gone to bed, looking for the dark hold of the room to swallow him. The chatter from below has stopped. He listens for a moment, then realises that his mother has taken Sully to her bedroom.

He lies back in his bed and tries to stop his mind following them, stop it from skimming across the living-room floor and slipping under their bedroom door like an all-seeing vapour. He tries to stop himself seeing their naked lust for each other. He puts his hands to his face to stop the tumble of images before his eyes. Sully's slimy lips sucking and licking at hers, his hard-arsed passion making her squeal in submission as his sweaty flesh slithers all over her moon-white skin.

He thinks of his deal with Teezy and tries to sleep, turning, dragging bedclothes this way and that. He remembers her eyes as she talked about Fintan. How her face had suddenly seemed young and open when she had told him her story. He thinks of his last contact with his father, when he had renounced him, and pushed his memory away as if it had been a plate of maggots. He thinks of the firefly, of the man in the alleyway. He thinks of his deaths and how stupid they seem. He suddenly feels terribly alone, and that the world is only what he sees and nothing more. There is no light above, no power beyond, no fireflies in the blackness of space; there had been no man in the alleyway. And as he falls towards sleep he feels a dark spear of fear nail him to the bed.

The Death of My Dreams

I feel so alone. Is this what it's like afterwards? To feel nothing, to be nothing? I want to die. I want her to stand over my grave and cry, to blame herself. I want her to rush to my dying body and beg my forgiveness. I want that to be the last thing I see, before I see no more. I want to see her beat Fathead Sully's chest as the last breath leaves my body. I want her to hold my bloody body and weep and know that I was the only one who truly loved her.

I am dreaming this. My sleeping body is tossing and turning, rolling in and out of different thoughts. It's a cold place, the end of your dreams. It's a black, horrible place where Nothing is king. I feel as if all the loneliness of a cruel world is flowing through my veins, and there is no one to catch me when I fall into darkness.

I hate my mind. I hate the way it runs and runs and runs like a wild horse. I can't keep up with it sometimes. It just drags me along behind it like the cowboys in the films who get caught in the stirrup of their horse and are bounced and bumped along until they die or are shot.

You used to stand at the end of my dreams, just like you stand in the photograph, that smile on your face, wearing that pinstripe suit just like a gangster, just like Al Pacino. But, like I told you the other night, I think you only exist in the emptiness of my mind, and it is you who frightens the wild horse into fleeing.

No, the fall at the end of my dreams is just that: a fall. And you are not there, like a guard, or a shiny policeman of light, to protect me. It is just a long fall into the dark kingdom where Nothing is king.

20. The Performance

He has never been on a stage before. At first it reminds him of the recurring dream that he began to have shortly after his father died, where he saw himself moving across a landscape of blackness, lit only by the fierce scrutiny of God's gaze. He remembers its heat on his skin, and he remembers trying to melt into the darkness that surrounded him.

It was a dream that had stalked his sleep for many years, and often he had woken in the middle of the night to find that he had wet the bed. He remembers fumbling with the wet sheets, running water through them in the bathroom, then praying that they would dry on the radiator overnight. So, when he makes his first entrance as Martini, shuffling to join the other inmates at the card table in the recreation ward, his heart rears in his chest and he feels as if he is walking across the flinty terrain of old dreams.

For a moment or two he hides behind Jarlath McAllister at the card table, but then something inside him charges his heart with courage. He thinks of the black jackdaw he had conjured on to his bedroom wall all those weeks before. Suddenly he feels a warmth seep into his soul, and slowly he begins to move across the territory of someone else's life.

Afterwards they huddle together in the women's dressing room, their hands reaching for each other, beating out congratulations on each other's shoulders. Shannon is in the middle of the mêlée and occasionally James sees his beaming face appear through the tangle of upraised arms and elbows. Eventually he is hoisted aloft and carried round the room on the men's shoulders, ducking now and then to avoid the coil of heating pipes and rails that run across the ceiling. Somebody claps James on the back and shouts, 'Bloody marvellous,' before diving back into the pack of celebrating bodies.

He refuses the wine that is being passed around in thin plastic cups. He thinks of the freedom he felt on the stage that night and wants more of it. He notices Kerry smiling at him, and looks away quickly, fumbling in his mind for something else to focus on. Then he realises she is walking towards him.

'Well done tonight, Jimmy.'

'Thanks.'

'Don't worry.' She places her hand on his arm. He notices how each finger bears a ring. Her hair is hidden beneath a heavy creamy turban. She reminds him of a fairground gypsy, a fortune-teller ready to peer into other people's lives.

'I'm not worried,' he says.

'Good. That's good.'

He senses she wishes to say something else, and is thankful that Chin Chin comes over, stands by her side and drapes a long arm across her shoulders.

'You were exemplary tonight, Master Lavery.'

'Thank you, Chin Chin.'

The three of them shuffle uneasily for a moment, peering down into their drinks.

'He's waiting for you to repay the compliment, darling.'

'Oh . . . Well done, Chin Chin.'

Later that night they all go dancing. Shannon leads the way and the rest follow, streaming out of the stage door of the opera house, breaking into song, their footsteps ringing noisily on the rain-black pavement. Chin Chin and Kerry walk behind the main group, their arms linked, big grins spread across their faces. James is glad he is free of her, free of her heavy touch and her cannibal's heart. They queue outside the Europa Hotel, waiting to be let through the security cage into the dance club beyond.

'Son.'

He is about to be searched by one of the hotel policemen when he hears Teezy call him, his arms raised in the crucifix position, the cop about to frisk him. He turns round, looks back down the street and sees her standing there with a small man who looks familiar. 'Teezy?'

He steps away from the queue, nodding an apology to the RUC man.

'Where you going, wee man?' he hears Jarlath shout.

'I'll follow you in, Jarlath. My auntie's here.'

'Well, don't be long, sunshine, we've some pulling to do.'

'Teezy, what are you doing here?' he asks, as he reaches her.

'Sam gave me a lift. You remember Sam, don't you?'

Sam Butler lives three doors from her: James often sees him on the street or about the town, walking his black Labrador, hat tilted on his head. He is always well turned out as if he is constantly going somewhere important.

'Hi, Sam,' James says.

'Young James.'

'Ah, son, I'm fierce proud of you, fierce proud.'

'Aye, son. You were magic so you were,' Sam says.

'Thanks. Why didn't you tell me you were coming, Teezy?'

'Ah . . . I didn't want you worrying yourself, son.'

'We're going for a drink, Teezy. Do you –'

'No, son, I won't. It's past my bedtime. Who'd have thought? You up on the stage all growed up and powerful-looking. Wouldn't have missed it for the world, son.'

They stand there looking at each other. He senses she wants to say something else, something that isn't easy for her.

'It's a pity mum couldn't have been there,' James says.

'Your mother has always been her own mind, son, you know that. Your mammy loves you in her own way, son. Anyway I'm here . . . Teezy's here.' She gives him a tight little hug, then looks at him for a moment, her eyes misting. 'My God, I'm proud of you.' Then she turns to Sam and says, 'Come on, then. Get me home, Sam.'

'Goodnight, young James,' Sam says.

'Goodnight.'

He watches them walk away, Sam's hand on Teezy's elbow as he leads her gently towards the nearby car park.

He joins the rest of the cast inside the nightclub. Everyone is on the dance-floor except Jarlath, who has found a gap at the crowded bar. James goes over to stand with him. They watch as the rest of the company move to the music, laughing at Shannon and Patricia, who look

176

as if they are trying to shake a colony of ants from their skin.

Jarlath offers to buy him a drink, but he asks for a Coke, weathering Jarlath's insistence that he have something stronger. 'What sort of a man are you?' Jarlath shouts above the din of the music, raising a pint of frothy Guinness to his lips.

He shrugs, and watches the gulp of Jarlath's Adam's apple as the Guinness slides down his throat.

'You're a strange one, Lavery,' he says, wiping the cream of his pint from his lips with the back of his hand. 'It's like you were possessed out there tonight – like a demon had got a hold of you – and look at you now. You wouldn't say boo to a goose.'

Jarlath goes off to hunt along the edges of the dance-floor, and James watches as he stops to chat with some young women, his pint spilling over the rim of his glass, his head dipping and weaving. James sips his Coke, and thinks once more of the warm womb of the stage that night, and of the fire that had run through his heart. He thinks of Teezy and the way her eyes had looked at him as if she were seeing him for the first time. He remembers the warm pride in her voice when she spoke to him.

He spends the rest of the evening jostling for space at the bar, guiding his glass back and forth as he is nudged and bumped. Eventually he gives up, fights his way to the exit and, with a sigh of relief, climbs the stairs that lead up on to the street. He is thankful of the cool air that hits his skin, and the damp drizzle that is falling. All around him he can hear the click of high heels on the pavements and the harsh shouts of rows beginning in alleyways. He looks at the thick-necked policemen as they frisk people, gruffly telling some of the drunker ones to behave. Some they let through the security cage with just a nod, young shaven-headed youths, all dressed the same way, in slacks and freshly pressed white shirts.

'No wonder this is the most bombed hotel in Europe.'

James looks round to see Cathal Murphy standing beside him, his cravat sodden with sweat, his forehead shiny and red.

'They're all squaddies . . . Brits.'

They're not much older than me, James thinks.

'I wouldn't say no to one or two of them.'

They look round to see Patricia standing behind them.

'Behave yourself,' Murphy says, as he tinkers with his cravat and runs a hand wearily across his shiny forehead.

'"There's no business like show business" . . . la di da.'

They turn to see Shannon standing behind them, steam rising from his large frame, his cheesecloth shirt unbuttoned to the navel.

'Lavery.'

'Yes, sir . . . Sean.'

'You acquitted yourself well tonight . . . quite – quite well.'

'Thank you, Sean . . . sir.'

'I, of course, was only marvellous.'

The four of them drive the forty-odd miles back to the border; Patricia sits in the front with Murphy, who is driving, James in the back with Shannon. During the journey Shannon sings and quips, plucking the ghosts of quotations and show tunes from the air, sipping hungrily from the large glass of *crème de menthe* he has smuggled from the club. Once or twice Shannon nudges him playfully in the ribs and performs a soliloquy directly into his startled face. They drop him off at the edge of his estate, Shannon squeezing the back of his neck playfully before he leaves the car. 'Keep fighting, Master Lavery, keep fighting.'

He waves goodbye as the car drive off to rejoin the main Dublin road, then turns towards his house. He lets himself in through the back door. He stands for a moment on its threshold, waiting for his eyes to grow accustomed to the darkness. Then he feels his way towards the living room, wincing as his leg catches the edge of the kitchen table.

He is almost in the centre of the living room when he sees Sully's silhouette sitting by the large window. He looks like a condemned man, his head drooping into his chest, his shoulders hunched. He doesn't look up or acknowledge that he has seen James. Then he says quietly, 'She's been saying his name in her sleep again.'

James stands watching as Sully folds his arms, then turns and looks James in the face. 'Ghosts, son, ghosts.'

James looks deep into the man's face. 'I'm going to bed,' he says.

'Be my friend, son.' Sully rises, his hands opened hopefully, his head moving in and out of night shadow as he edges forward.

'I said I'm going to bed.' James leaves the broken man in his capsule of grief and shadows, and slowly climbs the stairs to bed, calling in for a moment to look at the woman whose lips are parted in readiness for the ghost of a kiss.

Are You Receiving Me?

The Dream Bank
West of Pluto
In the Outer Solar System
Date: Not Applicable
Time: Even More Not Applicable

My son James,

This is a dream letter so the reception may be a little wonky. It is the only place I can seem to reach you these days. I am hurt. I have been hurt for a long time, but I'm not referring to that. I mean I am hurt because you have spent the last while trying to kill your dreams. When a man does that he truly begins to die. Look at Sully: he has no dreams – he thinks he has, but he killed them a long time ago, long before he met your mother. So, you see, he has nothing to offer her. All he can do is feed off her.

This is the only way I can seem to reach you now, and it is a bit shaky as a method, because the thing about dreams is that we rarely remember all of them. So I hope you remember the important parts. You have closed your heart to me. You are the expert on death: what does that say to you? It is a form of death, that's what it is, a form of murder, and probably the worst kind.

The thing about dreams, and the thoughts that make them up, is that we must accept them all, every single one of them. That's what makes us who we are. Well, I say 'we', what I mean is you. Obviously I am different now: my dreams are more real, where I am. Damn, I hate these things, dream letters. Some bright spark angel came up with them way back. I don't know how much of this you will remember – well, I suppose anything's better than nothing.

One more thing. If you kill your dreams, when

you die they all come back at once and there are so
many of them, and they are so angry at having been
stopped that they reappear as nightmares. I should
know. My allotted reception time is going. I love
you. Please keep dreaming.

Dad

21. The Reward

They are only minutes out of the harbour, the small ferry-boat chugging throatily out towards the island. The boys are huddled in small gangs on its deck, buttoned against the rising wind. James's hand rides the water, knuckle deep, little cuts and spits of waves tumbling up and down his arm. Plug hangs over the side of the boat beside him, his face the colour of white leather, his elbows hunched up, his head lolling in time to the swell of the boat. They have just left Burtonport, James thinks, and already there are casualties.

There are many boys on the boat who he has never seen before, boys from all over the North. Some had joined the coach on its journey that morning from Newry to the western tip of Donegal. Some had come on a separate coach, the ones, according to Plug, who were from Belfast. They number twelve or thirteen and move as a pack, their fists thrust into their green and black bomber jackets. Their leader is a tall boy, his head bone-shaved, and the rest of the gang take their promptings from him, shooting him nervous looks, like fidgety housewives.

Plug begins to vomit. James turns to look at him, biting back his own nausea as he watches chunks of vomit hit the sea, sitting on it like dense rice pudding before falling away into the depths.

'Are you all right?' James asks.

'Oh . . . eff . . .'

He sounds comical and pathetic. James laughs, bringing his hand up to his mouth to hide it from Plug.

'Up yours, Lavery.' He vomits again. There's less of it this time. After a while he rests his forehead on the rail, breathing heavily, his chest rising and falling.

'Is everything OK?' A young woman teacher has walked over to the boys and stands on the other side of Plug. She glances at James, then places her hand on Plug's back.

'He was sick, Miss.'

'Yes, I can see that. What's your name?'

'Mine?'

'Yes, yours.'

'James Lavery, Miss.'

'Maureen. My name is Maureen. You're not at school now. These are your holidays.'

184

'Yes . . . Maureen.'

She leans down to Plug's face and brings her hand up from his leather jacket to knead the back of his head with the tips of her fingers, James can see broken lines of fading varnish on her nails mingled with small calcium specks. 'Don't worry, we're almost there.' She looks at James once more, a smile on her lips, her hands joined as she tries to breathe some warmth on them. 'Where are you from?'

'Carrickburren, just outside Newry.'

'A border man.'

'Aye.'

James looks round at the Belfast boys who stand at the stern of the boat, their thin mouths tugging on cigarettes. A few blow kisses his way; one, a dark-eyed boy, just stares at him. James looks away, a chill spreading through his limbs.

The small harbour of Aranmore bustles with expectancy; children swirl round the pier like wind-tugged leaves. Fishermen wait for the ferry-boat to dock, some sitting on bollards, their legs thrust out, thin roll-ups dangling from their lips. Seagulls wheel in the air, their cries ringing off the harbour concrete.

A large café sits on the rise behind the harbour. James can see the wink of slot and pinball machines as the evening light fades. They disembark, testing their legs on the studded concrete. Old guy-ropes litter the quay like frayed snakes. They are herded towards an old school-house that sits about a quarter of a mile from the café. A few of the Belfast boys try to sneak in unnoticed, only to be retrieved by the largest of the supervisors, an impressive individual called Manus McManus.

James looks back at the harbour, at the people swarming round the ferry-boat, at the provisions being hurled from arm to arm, the fishermen's shouts competing with the harsh peal of the seagulls' cries.

Plug shuffles along beside him, the colour slowly returning to his cheeks. A line of girl students walk just ahead, giggling and pointing at Plug's sour-looking face.

'Oh, pee off, you horrible bunch.'

'They're only messin', Plug, only having a bit of fun.'

One of the girls, not much older than James, runs back and offers Plug her hankie. He doesn't take it but glares at her. James takes it and smiles, and for a moment they stay that way, smiling, not knowing when to look away. Then she turns and runs back to join her friends, her flouncing pigtails swallowed by a sea of bobbing heads. James shoves the hankie into Plug's hands. 'Here, you'd better take it.' He looks back but he can longer see her or her friends. Plug grabs the hankie and puts it to his mouth.

As they enter the school-house James thinks back to

186

earlier that day when he had stood with his mother and Sully as, all around him, boys had said goodbye to their parents.

'Call me, do you hear?'

'Yes.'

'Tonight, do you hear?'

'Yes.'

'That's a promise that me and God have both heard. OK?'

He hates it when his mother cries in public, like she had that morning as he stood waiting to board the coach, Sully standing discreetly to one side, his face turned away from them, pointedly giving them privacy.

'Muuuum!'

'Listen to your mother.' Sully had sounded as if he was in church, his voice thick with reverence, his eyes downcast as James's mother had delivered her sermon.

'Do you hear?'

'Yes, Mum.'

He had thanked God quietly that he was leaving when he was, and felt grateful to Teezy for finding the money for his holiday. After all, he had behaved, just as she had asked him to. He had pretended to himself and to the world that all was well, that God was in his heaven, that Sully was the model intruder, and that he hardly noticed that his world had ended. Yes, he had behaved. He had been the best he could have been because he knew a holiday lay at the end of the long road of his restraint, and with a holiday came escape.

Shortly after Sully's ghost episode, his mother had made a real effort, going dry for almost two months. James knew she was doing it only to soothe Sully, to stay in the land of the living with him and not disappear into the dark world that had so frightened him. It was in her eyes that James had noticed the greatest change. It was as if day after day a fine film of muddiness had been lifted from them. Sometimes he had stood and watched her as she sat by the window in the evenings as the light was fading, and was struck by how lonely she seemed, how small and vulnerable. She had begun drinking again two days before he was due to leave. He knew as soon as he had seen her. He had recognised it before he had smelt it. It was her eyes that had given her away.

In his first evening in the Gaelteacht he lies in bed and thinks of these things, and tries to quash the guilt he feels as he relishes his first day of freedom. At the school-house a few hours earlier they had been allocated their houses for the duration of their stay. Plug and he were to share one with four other boys from their school: Bubbles, a podgy boy who was in the year above them; Tom McAfee, a fuzzy-haired boy of their own age; Chink, an Asiatic-looking boy two years below them; and Alistair Geoghan, a small effeminate boy who was in the same year as Chink.

The next morning after breakfast the six walk the short distance along the coastline to the small school-house. Plug and James linger behind, watching the sea as it teems towards land, exploding in towers of spray. James loves the moment when the water is suspended, like a huge arced hand, before it crashes to the rocks.

Suddenly he stops and faces the horizon. He feels his face sheeted with a sudden spat of salt water. He closes his eyes and draws the sea to him, feeling it rush up like the ground on a ride at the fair. It is some moments before Plug realises he's been walking alone. Looking back he sees his friend standing on the point of the headland, his head tilted as if he were an orchestra conductor about to lead a symphony.

'Hey! Hey, head the effin' ball.'

Although he is only feet from James he has to lean into his shout. James ignores him. He raises his arms slowly so that they are perpendicular to his sides. Plug tries again: 'Hey, Lavery! We'll be scalped – we're late.'

'Close your eyes.'

'What?'

'It's fucking brilliant! Close your eyes.' He takes a step forward, feeling his plimsolls catch on a tuft of grass, and screws his eyes more tightly closed. He wonders how far he can go, how close he can get to the fall. He hears Plug screaming for him to stop, but he ignores him. He feels the wind tug at his armpits, as if it is saying it will

189

lift him, that it will give him wings. He smiles. He knows he is being sent a message, from the lights that circle heaven's gates.

As he takes his final step his legs buckle, as if they are shooting through a trapdoor, and his heart catapults into his mouth. Then he feels himself lifted, by two hands, clear of the drop. He is swung high in the air and dropped in a heap on the grass. 'What the fuck do you think you were doing, young man?'

He looks up into the eyes of Manus McManus. Then he sees how close he was to the drop.

'I'm waiting.' This time McManus prods his shoulder with a fist.

James looks up into the craggy face of his Irish teacher. 'What?'

'Don't fucking "what" me or I'll feed you to those bloody rocks. What's your name?'

'James.'

'James what?'

'Lavery.'

'Well, listen to me, James Lavery, and listen to me good.'

James notices Chink, Tom McAfee, Alistair Geoghan and Bubbles standing a small distance away, behind McManus, the hoods of their anoraks flapping in the wind like loosened tongues.

'Young man, have the common decency to look at me when I'm talking to you.'

'Sorry, sir.'

'If these lads here hadn't come and told me what was going on, by now we'd have been scraping you off those rocks down there with a long-handled shovel. Do you understand?'

James nods nervously. He looks at McManus's eyes: they seem to have softened.

'Get out of my sight, Lavery. And mark my words – I'll have my eye on you from now on.'

Word gets round his class. He is the boy who had tried to fly home, the seagull from South Armagh. Some of the girls make wing motions with their arms and squawk noises whenever he enters the classroom. One in particular, the young girl from the quayside the day before, comes up to him a couple of times and looks deep into his eyes. On one occasion he is standing with Plug in the garden outside the schoolhouse when she appears at his elbow. They stand quietly beside each other for some moments, before he dares himself to meet her upturned gaze.

'Wow,' she says. 'Wow.'

The Wow Letter

> *The Gaelteacht*
> *Arranmore*
> *Off the West Coast*
> *Of Ireland*

Hi, Dad,

*'Wow,' she said. 'Wow.' Did you hear her? Did the
word climb through the clouds and reach you, just
like the light from a torch that is shone at the moon?
We did it in physics. The light reaches the moon,
even though it is so far away, or at least some part
of it. I remember standing in the back garden
shining Mum's torch up into the faraway face of the
moon. I believed I was feeding light to you to keep
your strength up. Is it the same with words? Do
they all reach the ear of God at some point? Every
word that has ever been spoken?*

*I dreamed very strange things the other night,
pieces of dreams like a broadcast from a very
distant planet. It was you, wasn't it, trying to reach
me? I woke the next morning and it felt like*

someone had been singing me a soft, soft song in my sleep. I'm sorry I'm so confused. I know you shouldn't really be talking to me, and that sometimes God is angry with you. Dreams make things live, don't they?

'Wow.' No one has ever said that to me before. Is it a real word? I think it's in between, a dream-real word. I don't even know her name, but I suppose I have lots of time to find out. It is beautiful here, so wild and so free. Is that what heaven is like? I stood on the headland the other day and I knew you were there, far, far out in the hearts of the clouds, and in the beginning of the rain, I saw you, I saw your face. Everyone thinks I'm a bit crazy, but I don't mind.

Wow. Wow. Wow.

James

22. Her Name

Each day Manus McManus would send him for cigarettes. He would climb the long hill leading from the school-house to the grocer's shop on the main road, shooing the packs of farm dogs that patrolled the beaches and the roads. The shopkeeper, an old man with a drooping head, would hand over the Player's Navy Cut and speak Irish to him, watching with warm amusement as he struggled to reply. Eventually after three or four visits they talked in English, and James looked forward to his time with the old man, to the warm glow he would feel when he stepped into the shop.

One day the old man asks him to stay for a cup of tea. James hesitates, until the man says, 'There's time enough for everything, son.'

The tea is served by his wife, a small woman, who bows in and out of the parlour in little scuttles of deference.

'What's the rule about speaking Gaelic these days?' the old man asks.

'Er, what do you mean?'

'At the Scolaiste. Don't they have a three-strike rule?'

'Oh . . . yeah, if you're caught three times speaking English . . .'

'. . . you're sent home.'

'Yeah.'

As he leaves, the old man pats his arm, saying that they will see him the same time tomorrow, God willing. He thanks them for the tea, a blush warming his cheeks, and runs back to the school, the pack of farm dogs streaming behind him.

In the afternoons their time is their own, and they are free to wander the island, to explore its headlands and hidden beaches. Once or twice a week, though, there are some compulsory activities, that involve the whole of the island's students. These range from boat trips to nearby Tory island, or ping-pong and chess championships, or Ceilidh dancing lessons, in the grounds of one of the two school-houses.

It is at the chess and ping-pong championships that the Belfast boys make their reappearance. Rumours had been circulating for days at James's school about them. It had been said that one had cornered a girl, the one with the pigtails, the girl who had said 'Wow' to James a few days earlier, and made lewd suggestions to her, then laughed as she ran away. It had also been said that the smallest of the gang, a weasel-faced boy named Paddy, was beaten by the rest of them every evening, and treated with the same disdain as a boxing-club punchbag. Girls in James's class had attested to the sight of Paddy's broken skin and his plum-coloured bruises.

On this particular day there is no escaping them. James and his friends are being watched closely by Manus McManus, because they had not shown up at the previous chess and ping-pong championship a week earlier at the other school-house. They had preferred the quiet run of a nearby beach, tumbling in and out of the rasps of surf that had spilled on to the sand.

After the morning lessons with McManus, they had an hour for lunch. As they sat wolfing down their ham sandwiches, they speculated on what the afternoon would hold. Plug reckoned that at least three of the Belfast lot were on two warnings for speaking English and for general disobedience. He believed that because of this they might behave a little better. Alistair shouted that that was 'bollocks', just as the landlady, Rosie, came into the room with a fresh plate of sandwiches. Chink apologised for him. James suggested that they just keep to themselves, have a good time, and not give any of them an in. Bubbles, the largest of them, stood up, his sizeable belly quivering over his belt, and said, 'What the fuck?' and glared at them in turn, then sat down again.

'I agree with Bubbles,' Tom McAfee said.

'All he said was, "What the fuck?"' James pointed out.

'I know and I agree with him. What the fuck?' said McAfee.

The Belfast boys arrive late, just as the round robin games are beginning. Bubbles and James have been paired to play two boys from the other side of the island at ping-pong. Suddenly James realises they have an audience. The Belfast gang, newly arrived, stand in a line behind their opposition. He sees the little one, Paddy, standing slightly apart, a wide, palm-shaped bruise on his face, and a black and yellow ring beneath his left eye.

Suddenly the leader of the Belfast gang breaks away, pulling five or six boys with him in his wake; they shoal after him, like pilot fish bibbing a whale. James watches him as he strolls away, loose-limbed and threatening. The remaining Belfast boys shuffle sideways, filling the gaps their mates have left like soldiers on a parade-ground. The lean, dark-eyed boy that James remembers from the ferry trip is now directly opposite, glaring at him.

The match is a fiasco. Bubbles and James lose two games to zero. At one point they had both gone for the same return and crashed into each other, with James coming off worse, landing flat on his back, the jeers of the Belfast gang ringing in his ears. At the end of the game Bubbles hurled his bat down on the table, shouting, 'Fuck it,' at the top of his voice.

'*As Gaelige, as Gaelige,*' one of the teachers warns him.

He refuses to shake hands with the victors and storms off down the recreation hall. James does shake hands. They smile at him; he doesn't smile back.

The next ping-pong foursome dive on the bats and begin to warm up. James leaves the room and goes outside to look for Plug and the others.

'Cathleen. My name is Cathleen.'

He hasn't seen her follow him. It takes him by surprise and he just stares at her.

'Don't worry, I won't do the seagull thing.'

He smiles, and wills himself to speak but all he can manage is 'Wow.'

'You were funny in there, the way you were bouncing off your friend. Too bad you didn't win.'

'Bubbles.'

'Is that his name?'

'I didn't like the other two. They were a bit poncey.'

'Yeah.'

For a moment they look at each other, and then she smiles quietly.

'Well, well, well. Who'd have thunk it?'

James turns to see a few of the Belfast boys ringing

them, the dark-eyed boy looking him directly in the eyes. He flicks a look to Cathleen and grins. 'Remember us, Miss Prissy?'

James remembers the story he had heard, of how they had cornered her the other night, undressing her with their smutty remarks. He looks at Cathleen and sees the light stall in her eyes. 'Piss off.' As he says it, he steers Cathleen away and walks them both in the direction of the school-house, his legs tingling viciously with nerves.

The first blow gets him squarely between the shoulder-blades, causing him to lurch forward, his legs buckling like those of an unsteady foal. He desperately spreads them and trying to turn, meets the next blow full in the face. He hears Cathleen shout and sees her peel away to one side. He hears the dark-eyed boy snort as he ploughs his boot into his backside.

The ground when it meets his face is damp; he feels its wetness spread across his cheek. He rolls on to his back. He can see a crowd has begun to gather, closing him in like a pig in a pen. He looks around for Cathleen, but can't see her any more. He sees his attacker hovering above him, his fists held loosely at his hips, a look of disgust on his face. He knows that he must get up. He must respond. Honour demands it. His body quakes as every cell, every molecule in him goes to war.

When he is half-way to his feet he lunges at his opponent, and his fists start smashing their way into the other boy's face. He enjoys the feeling, the pure thrill of striking back, of inflicting pain, of kicking against what life has dealt him. The other boy grabs him by the hair, trying to pull his head down towards his boots. James's hands move to his attacker's throat, grabbing at his Adam's apple. For a while they stay that way, shuffling together like two old men in the dirt. In the end his opponent's greater bulk begins to tell and they hit the ground and roll, with the Belfast boy scrambling to sit astride him, his knees pinning James's arms to the ground, his wide fists landing blows in his face. They are pulled apart like two warring dogs. McManus holds the Belfast boy by the gathered neck of his T-shirt. James is restrained by Maureen and a male teacher called Liam.

They both receive a public warning. The Belfast boy has already received two and is told he will be on the first ferry to the mainland. He takes the news with an unblinking defiance. McManus shoves the boy away from him with a dismissive thrust of his arm, and strides over to James, calling on the crowd of onlookers to disperse as he does so.

'He started it,' James says, before his teacher can speak, dancing from one foot to the other. Cathleen, who is standing behind him now, brings out a handkerchief and offers it to him; it appears over his shoulder out of nowhere, causing him to start. McManus takes the hankie from her and applies it to James's lip.

'He started it.'

A couple of times James looks at Cathleen and sees himself there, in her eyes, his face rounded with enquiry and hope. She smiles at him and gently shakes her head in a show of sympathy, and a spark of something that James can hardly dare to believe is respect.

Errol Flynn Says He's Proud of Me

News from Heaven, or space, I should say. Errol Flynn told my father that he was proud of me. He said that I had behaved with great chivalry. He said that of course there had been no swords because the rules of fighting for a woman's honour had changed. Now it was not only fists but feet and knees. He told my father that he couldn't believe how dirty my opponent had been. But he said honour won the day. He said that my burst of punches would have made the finest heavyweight in the world proud, and that my opponent didn't stand a chance after that, even though he had got me on the ground. He said it would only have been a matter of time before his brain gave up.

'Wow.' I've been using that word a lot recently. It's a special word. I believe it has magic, because my life has changed since I first heard it.

My father said that at first he didn't realise it was Errol Flynn because he was moving so fast, speeding by like a shooting star, my father said. Also he said he didn't think that Errol was up there with his lot, because of things that had happened in Errol's real life. But Errol told him that he had only recently been let up there and that was why he was moving so fast – in case they changed their mind.

He said the best kinds of fights are over women, because of the reward. I haven't had mine yet, but that's not why I did it – well, maybe a little bit.

Anyway, 'Wow.'

23. The Captain

The next few days pass like scenery from a moving train, breathtaking and filled with seeing. James barely thinks of his promise to phone his mother, and when he does he ignores it, burying it beneath the gusts of excitements those next ten days bring him. The only time it is difficult for him is if he accompanies Plug to the local phone box, and sees the line of kids queuing to phone home.

He stood one night waiting for Plug for close on an hour, watching him through the heavy plate glass of the phone box as he relayed the events of the past few days to his parents, events that they had shared together. One or twice he felt for change in his pocket, but something always stopped him. He knew he still couldn't forgive her for letting Sully move in, and the thought of the man in his house made his skin crawl.

He was now Cathleen's hero. A position he relished. They spent more and more time together. Sometimes they walked for hours on the bumpy headlands and the soft beaches. He felt awkward and shy around her, and loved the electric jag in his heart every time he looked at her. For days their only language was silence, and they would stand and face the sea, both believing they could see every dream they'd ever had rising on the waves.

'Have you done it yet?'

'What?' James asks.

'You know,' Plug says, squinting his eyes into a leer.

'No, I don't know.'

It is the end of the day. Plug and he are walking back to their house along the coastline.

'With what-do-you-call-her?'

'She's got a name.'

'Yeah. What do you call her? Whingey?'

'Her name's Cathleen.'

'Who cares?'

'What's your problem, Plug?'

'No problem.'

Suddenly they see an old man standing on the point of the headland just below their house. It is some moments before James realises it is Seamus the grocer. In his right hand he holds a sack, his hand bunched into a fist round its neck. The bag is moving – whatever is inside is thrashing around.

'*Dia dhuit*, Seamus.'

'*Dias Muire dhuit*, James.'

The old man looks away almost as soon as he returns the greeting.

'What's in the bag?'

'The Captain.'

Captain was his dog, a collie. Every time James had gone to visit the old man to buy Manus's cigarettes the dog had lunged at him playfully, his neck mane ruffled with excitement. James had noticed that the dog's back legs were always stiff, and sometimes made it look a little comical because it carried them as if they were fused together, hopping after James as he left the shop every day.

'What are you going to do with him, Seamus?'

'Drown him.'

James thinks of the dog inside the sack. He sees what he thinks is the outline of a brick. He imagines the look of confusion and betrayal in the dog's eyes. He hears it yelp as it tries to break free of the bag. 'Don't, Mr Seamus.'

'Yes, don't, Mr Seamus.'

They look to each other, each egging the other to speak, to do something.

'I'm sorry, lads, but it's the way of things. He's finished. No use to me any more.'

The two boys bow their heads. James quietly thuds his foot on the wiry grass of the headland.

'We'll take him, Seamus,' James says.

The old man looks at him, and shakes his head. 'No, son. You have a good heart but he's finished. I have a new one at home, so eager she'd take your hand off. I can't afford two – especially not one whose legs have gone. No, this is the way. No more pain. No more struggles.'

Plug tugs at James's sleeve, but James can't look at him. He keeps his head bowed, trying desperately to stem his tears. He looks at the sack, at the old man holding it, and storms off towards the house, the dog's yelps rising pathetically behind him.

'Hey!'

He can hear Plug's cries rise behind him, and his feet as they pound after him.

'Hey!'

He stops and turns to face his friend, his eyes red from crying. 'What?'

'What the hell is wrong with you, Lavery?'

'Mind your own, Plug.'

'That stupid cow has you daft.'

'Fuck off.'

'You've been sleppin' after her like a poodle for the last week and your brain's gone mushy.'

'Piss off.'

'I bet she hasn't even let you kiss her yet. She's just a fucking tease.'

They look at each other, both taking a moment for what has just happened to sink in. Then Plug says, 'Look what you made me do, you bastard. You made me fucking curse.'

Death of a Friendship

The Kingdom of Arranmore
Donegal, Ireland

Count Plug,

You are nothing more than a shark looking for its next prey. You are lower than a snake; you are less than good. I will not put up with what you said about my queen. I will not tolerate it; I will not hear her slandered.

I can't believe what you said to me about her. After all we have been through, all the battles for our dear country against the arrogant English and sometimes even our own countrymen. I have loved you like a brother or like the father I never had, and this is the thanks I get.

I have decided I will cut you from my heart. I don't need anyone else but her. She is my light. She is my ace of hearts. If necessary I will fight you for the things you have said, I will cut your heart from your body and leave it bleeding on the harbour pier.

My queen says that you are jealous, that you resent what we have found together. People change, that's what I say, people move on and everyone must find their queen. I can't believe you are not happy for us. My fist in your mouth will soon sort that out.

So this is for you, Count Plug of the Carrickburren lowlands. Death to our friendship, death to our brotherly love, and death to you if you insult fair Cathleen once more.

Because, as both you and I know, in the films the hero always gets the girl.

Farewell.

Baron James O'Lavery
Overlord of the South Armagh Warriors

24. The Last Night

In the three days that are left James does not go back to Seamus the grocer's for Manus's cigarettes, preferring the longer journey to the newsagent on the far side of the island. He blames the old man for what he did to his dog, refusing to believe that it had been the only option. Plug and he never talk about the incident, or their words afterwards, but both events sit between them like a heavy stone. They spend more time apart, enjoying the company of their other friends, Plug preferring to go for long walks with Chink and Tom McAfee to discuss next year's school term, James spending more time on his own or with Cathleen.

On the final night there is a *céilí* on the far side of the island. The six boys walk the two miles or so, quietly watching the stars appear like necklaces of icy bullets in the sky.

James thinks of Cathleen and their last walk together the previous evening. They had met on the broken wall about a half-mile from the grocer's. He remembers how night had been falling, and how she had walked towards him out of the gathering gloom as if she owned it. They had walked the dusty roads, as always in silence, he slightly behind her. At one point she had turned and faced him. 'Tomorrow is our last night. What do you think of that?'

'Yeah,' he had softly replied.

'We should make it special . . . tomorrow night.'

'Yeah.'

For a long time they had looked at each other. Eventually he broke it, turning to pluck at a wind bush.

'Is something wrong?' she asked him.

'No,' he had said quickly.

'You think too much, James Lavery.'

At that point she had put her hand to his face. It was their first touch. It thrilled his heart.

James and Bubbles are the first to enter the dance hall, pushing their way through the lines of locals and students that ring the floor. Up on stage an old man sits on a steel-framed chair playing the accordion. James edges ahead of Bubbles until he reaches the makeshift lemonade bar. A young girl tends it, hurriedly collecting the empties, draining them into a large bin of slops, then plunging them into a bucket of soapy water. 'Yeah?'

'A Coke . . . please.'

'No Coke left.'

'Lucozade, then.'

'No Lucozade either.'

'What do you have?'

'Brown lemonade or white.'

'OK.'

'Which one?'

'Brown – no, white.'

He grabs his lemonade, pays for it, and makes his way back to the main body of the dance-floor.

'Well, Master James.'

He turns to find himself facing Manus.

'How are things?'

'Good, sir.'

'Glad to hear it, James. Are you looking forward to getting home?'

'Yes . . . Sort of.'

'You're not going to flap your way back, are you?' He makes a half-hearted bird motion with his arms.

'No, sir.'

'Well, take good care of yourself, Lavery – and keep up the Irish.' He pats James's shoulder, then lets his hand rest there a moment. 'Thanks for the cigarettes. And maybe see you next year.' He winks at him, then leaves, placing his untouched lemonade on the ticket desk. James watches him go.

Later that evening Cathleen comes up and stands beside him. They watch a crowd of kids dancing the 'Waves of Tory'. All the while he can feel her closeness as they watch, as if she lay in the pathways of his breathing. On-stage the accordion player has been joined by a fiddler, and they begin to play a waltz.

Cathleen puts her arm on his. 'Let's dance. After all, it is our last night.' She steers him out on to the dance floor, and drapes her arms round his neck, her hips swaying slowly in front of him, encouraging him to follow suit. 'Relax. I'm not going to bite you.'

He begins to move with her, feeling his body edge towards hers, until he feels the sporadic bump of her hips against his thighs.

'What's wrong?'

'Nothing.'

She edges her hands across the small of his back, lacing them together so that he feels sewn to her, hip to hip, groin to groin. 'Do you fancy a walk?' he says suddenly.

She looks up at him, her eyes glazed with the lilting seesaw of the waltz. 'OK.'

They walk along the headland where Seamus the grocer had dispatched Captain. He tells her of the episode with the dog, of the buckling of the sack, of the sharp edge of the brick jutting through the cloth, of the old man's face, the hard matter-of-factness in his eyes.

They pass the headland and walk along the arm of the coast, clambering down a jagged patch of rocks to reach a small hidden beach, made silver by the moon. They stop and watch the outgoing tide, their arms linked. Then she turns and faces him. 'James Lavery, I've waited a week for this.'

When she kisses him, she stands up on her toes, her eyes closed, and her lips parting to welcome his. He feels the childlike thread of her breathing mingle with his, and tastes the soft prayer she offers him.

'You're owed that, Mr Lavery, for being my hero.'

He walks her home. After a week of silence and shyness they begin to speak. She tells him that she believes in reincarnation and that people meet each other for a reason, and that nothing in God's world happens by chance. She tells him that she believes she was a bird in a previous life. She says a fortune-teller had told her she would have three children, one of each. She laughs playfully as she makes her joke, her tongue coming to rest teasingly between her teeth.

'You know, I thought there was something wrong with you.'

'What do you mean?' he asks.

'Well . . . you wouldn't touch me or anything. I thought you were . . . you know . . .'

'What?'

'You know . . .'

'No way.'

Between their final goodnight kisses they promise to stay in touch, to write to each other as soon as they reach home, and for him to come and see her in Dublin. He walks away from her cottage. He looks back to the doorway where they had parted. He imagines her undressing. He sees her standing naked in his thoughts, like the promise of sun in winter.

The next morning he joins the rest of the students at the small pier on the far side of the island. Suitcases are loaded on to the waiting ferry by fishermen, who bark instructions to one another over the gurgling of the engine and the screeching of panicked gulls. The sky is heavy with cloud, and a wind blows in off the sea. He looks nervously about the pier, hoping to see her before he goes.

He feels angry that his time on the island is at an end. He spits on the ground and feels some of the moisture spray back on to his cheek. When he thinks no one is looking he brings his hand to his face and wipes it off.

'Good morning.'

He turns his head to see her standing before him, and blushes as he wonders if she has seen his pathetic mess of a spit. 'Morning.'

It all sounds so mundane, as if they are meeting for the first time and all the fiery things they had said and done the night before are nothing more than smoke.

'Did you sleep?' she asks.

'Kind of.'

'Me too.'

'I'll call you.'

'You'd bloody better.' She skips forward and places a fleeting kiss on his lips, then moves away from him in the direction of the café, her head cocked, her eyes laughing gently at him. 'Give me a call, James Lavery.'

This time the ferry journey seems shorter, the sea passing by the side of the boat like a long grey soup. The students are subdued, gazing back at the island as it recedes. Rain has begun to fall. They dock in Burtonport. Manus organises them, roughly guiding them off the boat, delivering barked instructions in Irish. As James passes him, the teacher tousles his hair and winks at him. '*Slan leat*, James.'

'*Slan*, Manus.'

For a moment James stands on the pier and looks in the direction of the island, trying to see it one last time through the mist. The rain is falling more heavily now, hammering the surface of the sea with small, bullet-like explosions. People start to disperse, scurrying towards the waiting coaches. He turns up his collar and moves towards the Newry coach. On his way he suddenly stops.

Manus is standing with a smaller man; there is something about him that looks familiar.

He watches as Manus looks around the pier, his eyes running over every student who passes. Once or twice James can feel his tutor's eyes, and wonders why he hasn't seen him, as he is sure that the man with his back to him is Sully, and that the student they are searching for is him. He walks towards them, the rain smacking harshly on his forehead.

It is Manus who sees him first. He inclines his head towards the man beside him and spits a few words out of the side of his mouth. The man turns abruptly in James's direction, and James sees immediately that he was right: it is Sully.

When he reaches them, they stand in silence for a few moments. Sully, he realises, can't look at him. Eventually Manus speaks: 'Mr Sullivan has something to tell you, James.'

Sully nods, and for the first time looks straight into James's eyes. He has been crying. 'It's your mother, James.'

No One Is Talking to Me

Is this what it is like? To be dead? To be no longer a part of things? You see, no one is talking to me. No one is saying a word. I'm trying not to panic. Just like Al Pacino in The Godfather, *I'm trying to stare down the news I see in their eyes. Or, like John Wayne in* Stagecoach, *I'm trying to be brave, and face everything with only my rifle and my horse. That's all I need. Or maybe I'm King Arthur and I know God's mind and I accept everything with a kingly smile. Or I'm Errol Flynn and all I have to do is swashbuckle my way out of this.*

No, no one is talking to me. Sully is standing in front of me, and his eyes are red, and he looks so small and stupid. Manus just stares at the ground as if his head has got too heavy for his shoulders. So is this what it is like? Is this the way people stare into a coffin, with that frightened look in their eyes?

'It's your mother, James.' That's all that has been said. Not 'Jimmy' or 'young man'. Not even 'kid'. No, the serious grown-up 'James', and that frightens me.

No, I'm Al Pacino, like the day when Sully laughed at me, but he got his comeuppance when he was garrotted in his van for questioning the family. Yes, I'm Al Pacino. I don't even feel the rain, and I don't care about anything – I don't even care for that woman I've just met. I've forgotten who played her in the film – Diane something . . . Keaton. That's it.

No, no one is talking to me. Well, let them. I'm used to it.

25. The Checkpoint

Just before the checkpoint at Strabane, Sully mistimes the clutch, noisily forcing the car into second gear. They crawl along in a queue of cars, waiting to be checked by the soldiers and the RUC, who stand guarding the border. James gazes out of the window. He sees the reflection of his eyes. They glare back at him, daring him to cry. For the past hour they have driven in silence, broken only by the sweep of the wipers, or the perky blink of an indicator, the car swishing along the roads.

Just before they had set off from Burtonport, Sully and he had sat in the car, gazing out at the rain. He had watched as Sully had turned towards him, awkwardly swivelling in the seat to get a better look at him. 'Listen, kid, your mother has had an accident.'

James had listened as Sully explained that she had become more and more erratic since he had left for the Gaelteacht. She had begun drinking round the clock every day, failing to go into work, sitting in her front room, surrounded by dirty plates and empty glasses. He told him how she had cursed her son for not calling.

She had insisted on calling Sully by her dead husband's name, Conn, her eyes brimming with taunts. He told him of how he had called the doctor and of how the two men had considered sectioning her, but in the end Sully said he couldn't do that to her. So he slipped sleeping pills into her food when she thought to eat, carrying her to bed when she went under, hoping a long sleep would turn her round.

Instead when she woke she had sealed her mouth to him, leaving him only her eyes, which followed his every move, accusing him with their fuck-you glare.

One night he said he had left her to it, heading to the club for a few drinks with his mates. He told James he had left her gazing out of the window, holding a piece of the curtain free of the glass. When he had asked her who or what she was looking out for, she had lowered her head in frustration as if someone had just walked in front of a movie she was been watching.

He told James that when he had returned to the house in the early hours of the next morning, he had been struck immediately by the silence. All the lights were off, and the garden gate was swinging on its rusting hinges.

He had told James he knew instantly that something was wrong. He had put his key into the front-door lock and as he had pushed the door forward he had felt the resistance of a bulk on the other side. He reached in and hit the light switch. At first he had thought that the coat-stand had fallen forward, but then he had realised it was Ann, lying collapsed in the doorway.

He told James of the blood on the walls of the hallway and the back of the door. He described the doll-like bundle of his mother's body. He spoke of fumbling with her slashed wrists trying to find a pulse. He told him of his relief and anger when he did find one. Finally he had told James of the haste of the hospital staff to put blood back into her. He had told him of the long hours at the hospital waiting for news, pacing its corridors, looking hopefully into the faces of passing doctors and nurses.

After the first critical night he was eventually told that she had lost a lot of blood but that she would recover. He said he had cried, and tears began to fall as he had recounted this to James. At this point, though, James had already removed himself, turning to look out of the window, his eyelids drooping from the heaviness of the news he had just heard.

'Your driving licence, please, mate.'

James turns his head to see Sully grapple with his coat pocket as he tries to locate it.

James looks at the young soldier and the RUC man behind him whose eyes flit menacingly around the car.

'Are you all right, son?' The policeman leans in over the soldier's shoulder, his pale green eyes squinting slightly. James doesn't say anything, but just stares back at him.

Sully sees the hard look between them. 'Sorry, but he just had some bad news.'

'Is that right?' the policeman says.

'Yeah. His mother has been admitted to Daisy Hill in Newry. I'm bringing him there now.'

'Right. What's the name?'

'Mine?'

'No, we have yours – it's on the licence. His.'

'Lavery, James Lavery.'

The cop frowns as Sully answers for James, causing his peaked cap to rise up his forehead. 'Ever been in any bother, James?'

'No . . . no bother.'

'Are you his parrot?'

'Listen, I'm sorry but he really has had some awful news. His mother tried to harm herself a few days back. He's just found out. So . . .'

The cop looks once more at James and then stands upright, pulling his upper body out of the window frame. 'Go on. On your way.'

A Letter to God

On the Road
Somewhere Between Strabane
And Newry
Northern Ireland

Dear God,

I don't believe in you. You don't exist. I don't believe
that you see everything and know everything and have
all power. Who do you think you are? You just let us
scrabble around down here like ants or like children
who have lost their way. You probably spend your
time laughing at us with all your shitty angels and
stupid saints. Yes, it's probably a bloody good laugh
watching us make such a mess down here.

How could you let her do this? And why do you
make me feel as if I am to blame? You see, you're
making me talk to you as if you were there. You're
not. You never were.

Not Signed

26. The Man of Light

His mother's face is pale. Her hair is damp with perspiration; it lies in long, matted fingers on her forehead and down her neck. Aunt Teezy stands on watch by her bed. Sully has retreated after leading James to the side of the bed, putting distance between him and his lover's torn body.

The staff nurse, who had brought them in, a young portly woman, stands by James, her hand resting in the small of his back. She explains to James that his mother has lost a lot of blood, that she is under sedation, and that when she is well enough her care and rehabilitation will continue in some form or another. She says that it is such a terrible thing and that he is being very brave, that he is such a handsome, caring son.

He feels nothing: the words of the nurse and the small snuffled 'Good boy' that Teezy offers his way fall like half-hearted rain on his ears. He is divorced from what is happening, as if he has wandered into someone else's family.

She opens her eyes a few times while he is there and stares at him, her yellow lips moving as if she is still chewing the remains of food that has long since reached her gut. 'Conn?'

His mother has turned her head towards him and is calling him by his father's name. He realises that she is looking at him but isn't seeing him, and that her eyes seem to be following a shadow that lies across his face, a shadow that he knows only he and she can feel. Sully takes a step forward, clears his throat, and asks her if she needs anything, but Teezy stops him mid-sentence, placing her hand on his arm. James watches as Sully slowly bows his head, unable to look at her. He follows the track of her eyes as it moves from his face past the plastic and steeled-tube chair and the small exit sign above the ward double doors, until her head rests in profile, her eyes fixed dead ahead.

Slowly, as if forming out of the fluorescence of the overhead strip of light, a shape like a long tablet of shadow and light begins to gather definition. It seems to twitch and quiver like a slowly hatching pupa. First he sees the long shanks of its thighs, then the sweep of its back and the soft curl of the biceps. He senses Teezy look his way, mild panic rising in her eyes. The figure is now inches from his mother's body. James knows that only he and she can see the man of light who holds her body prisoner. He watches as every living part of her strains upward towards it, her breasts, her chin, her hips.

'Is she having a fit?' Teezy asks.

'No.'

He can feel Sully and Teezy look over at him as he says this, but he is beyond them, watching as his mother's bandaged arms rise tentatively from the borders of the bed and form the beginnings of an embrace.

That night he stays with Teezy, watching wordlessly as she prepares them supper. Now and then he can sense her watching him, as if he is an injured cat or dog. They eat in silence, their knives and forks scraping across their plates. Eventually James gives up, pushing away his plate, turning to gaze out of the window.

'You must eat. You'll need your strength.'

'I'm not hungry.'

'That's no good to your mother.'

'I'm not hungry.'

'How was your holiday?'

He gets up and goes to sit in the living room at the front of the house. He thinks of his mother lying in the hospital ward. He thinks of all the times he has been angry with her, how he has wanted to punish her for her silences, to scream at her to give his father the decency of a shared memory. He also thinks of the times he felt sorry for her, leading her unsteady body to bed and clearing the house of drink. He now sees there was no room in her heart for him, that it was swollen from the loss that had dogged her for years. He sees that his father lived there, that she had kept him prisoner, refusing to let him die, and in doing so had begun to die herself.

He sees her lying in the sterile cocoon of the hospital ward, her face offered to the light-filled man who hovers above her, the breath tumbling from her lips as she tries to impart life to him or to join him in death.

Letter to the Man of Light

Teezy's House
The Centre of Newry
Opposite McDowell's
The Newsagent

Dear Man of Light,

Is that what you've been doing to me too? Keeping me prisoner all these years? Tying me up in your light beams, making me believe in your memory

*even if it hurt my heart and stopped me living? Is
that what heaven is like, full of beings of light
waiting to be asked back?*

*Are you really my father or are you just what my
mother and I want you to be? Is it hard to be
always with us, unable to sleep, unable to fly past
in a whoosh like Errol Flynn did last week?*

*You have always been here, haven't you? And it
isn't natural, is it? It isn't something you should be
doing, is it? Why haven't you gone? It's not only
because we haven't let you, is it? It's because somewhere you don't want to. Somewhere you don't
want to believe you're dead, do you?*

*Teezy doesn't know what's going on. She thought
Mammy was having a fit today, and I thought Sully
was going to cry, he looked so tiny and scared. But
we know what's going on, don't we?*

*I have to say, it frightened me a little to see you
today. You looked so big and angry and you were
lying across Mammy as if you wanted to stop her
breathing. But then I thought about it and I realised
that you would never hurt her because you are lost
like us, and the same light that made you made me
too.*

*Best wishes,
James*

27. God Has a Plan for Us All

Sully calls round later that evening, his head first peering round the door jamb as if he is unsure he has the right house. For a moment he stands in the middle of the floor gently opening and closing his raincoat to tease the rain from it. He then shuffles to the seat by the fire, a tiny sigh of relief falling from his lips as he sits. 'Your mammy's out. Fast asleep.' He gazes at the fire, his profile cutting into the dancing shadows of the flames, like an axe finding its mark. 'The doctor says to let her sleep.' As he says this he looks at James and nods.

Teezy brings him a cup of tea, offering it to him tenderly as if he is a child freshly restored from a tantrum.

'Have you anything stronger, love?'

James leaves them to it. He pulls his coat from the

airing cupboard on his way out and feels for the telephone number he knows is stowed in the inside pocket.

'Where are you going, son?'

'Out.'

The rain has stopped, and the buildings and pavements glisten like wet liquorice under the street-lights.
He kicks a beaten beer can along for a while, toying with
it, enjoying the sound of its angry clatter in the empty
street.

His fingers tremble as he dials her number. A couple
of times he stops and replaces the receiver, holding his
hand on it as he summons the courage to redial. He
moves to another phone box and this time feeds the
coin into the slot, his voice cutting across the beeping
hiatus, so for a moment he thinks he's been cut off.
Eventually a dark, steady voice at the other end repeats
his hello.

'Hi . . . hello?'

'Yes?'

'Er . . . is Cathleen there?'

'Not at the moment, no. She's gone out.'

'Oh.'

'Who's calling?'

'A friend . . . er, James.'

'Can I take a message, James?'

'Yes. Could you say . . . er . . . James called?'

The man laughs at the other end of the line, a deep

telephone crackly laugh that unnerves James, prompting him to slam down the receiver and jump from the telephone box, wiping his palms along the sides of his anorak.

For a moment he stands and looks at it. He draws a long spit up his throat and fires it at the muddy glass of the booth and watches as it mingles with the tracks of rain. 'Fuck.'

He walks up Nurse's Hill, thinking of the face Cathleen offered to him only two nights before, her eyelashes quivering with anticipation as he had bent to kiss them, her mouth softly stung from the heavy wetness of his mouth. He wonders where she is, what she's doing, if she remembers their embraces.

How remote the island now seems. He thinks of it sitting in the cold embrace of the Atlantic Ocean, the spectres of their kisses swirling around its salt-driven roads, pooling in the quiet corners of its fields, like storm-driven butterflies, their delicate wings quivering forlornly. He vows to call again tomorrow, to brave the thick challenge of what must have been her father's voice. He feels a shiver of embarrassment sweep up his spine as he remembers the tease of the man's laugh, and as he climbs the steep hill towards the hospital his mind twists it into a deep, patronising guffaw.

'Son, you're soaked.'

'Yeah.' He says it almost as a challenge, looking straight into the concerned eyes of the ward sister, his hair hanging in rain-plastered lines across his forehead, his hands bunched in his anorak pockets.

'Here, take that sopping thing off you.'

'I want to see my mum,' he says.

'All in good time, son, all in good time.'

Delicately she loosens the coat from his back and holds it away from her, a small pool of water growing on the corridor floor. She grins at him and slowly shakes her head. 'We'll have you in the next ward if you're not more careful.' She brings him a towel and watches as he dries his hair. He feels the friction of the rubbing bring some warmth back to his scalp and into his hands. She then offers him a blanket and leads him to his mother's bed through the fridge light stillness of the ward. 'I shouldn't really be doing this, you know.'

His mother is asleep, her face partially hidden by hitched-up blankets. He pulls a chair up to the bedside and sits.

'She's had a quiet night. She even ate some pudding and drank a cup of tea. Speaking of which . . .'

He doesn't look as the ward sister goes off, but hears the squeak of her plimsolls on the tiled floor.

He looks around the ward at the white mounds of sleeping bodies, and hears the soft snores of one or two. One old woman across from him is awake and stares at him, her arms folded about her hospital gown. Someone coughs.

He stares at his mother. He looks at the bandages that

231

cover her arms, ragged emblems of her fight against herself. He sees her small empty hands peep out from beneath them, her fingers bent into her palms, her thumbs hidden from view. He thinks of her lying in the dark hallway at home before Sully found her, her ripped wrists offered skywards.

'Here you are.' The ward sister stands beside him and watches as he lifts the cup to his mouth, a faint smile crossing her lips. 'You have her mouth,' she says.

He stops drinking, rests the cup on the saucer and brings the back of his hand up to his mouth, hiding it momentarily from her eyes.

'Now, will you be all right if I leave you for a while?'

'Yeah. Thanks.' He notes her fresh round face, and the freckles on the bridge of her small nose.

'Don't worry. God has a plan for us all,' she says. She retakes her position at her station at the entrance to the ward and smiles over at him.

He smiles back, half-heartedly lifting his arm to emphasise the sincerity of it.

'Conn?'

His mother has opened her eyes and is looking directly at him, her lips parted, her tongue resting against her bottom teeth. The air around him seems to buzz as if a sudden flood of electrical power has seized it. He shifts uncomfortably in his seat and tries to speak, but something dries the words in his mouth.

She gently rocks her head from side to side as if trying to shake a heavy foreboding free of her mind, her lips opening and closing. Once again she says his father's name. He sits transfixed; he can feel his heart thud heavily in his chest. The hospital ward falls away, everything seems to stop. The only thing he sees is the fever in his mother's eyes.

'I'm sorry, Conn.' This time her voice is stronger and hot with rising tears. James feels a shadow touch his face and move across it like an invisible hand. Suddenly she tries to sit, her bandaged arms shooting down by her sides as she raises her torso. 'Don't go – you promised me. You fucking promised me.'

James can feel a light begin to burn on his face like the heat of a hurricane lamp. It seems centred on his cheek, a fierce insistence running from the centre to his jaw line. He brings his hand up hurriedly to his face, and in that moment he feels as though he is caressing the burning glow of his father's restless soul.

The ward sister has returned. He doesn't realise it until he sees her scrubbed hands begin to coax his mother into lying back, clasping her firmly by the shoulders and easing her down into the folds of the bedcovers.

'I think it's perhaps an idea if you left her to me for a while, son.'

He looks at his mother's face, peaceful now that sleep has claimed it, and back to the sister, his eyes holding hers.

'Don't worry, she'll be fine. She's in good hands. Go on, get some sleep.'

It is well after midnight when he arrives back at Teezy's and, to his surprise, she lets him in before he has a chance to knock. She tells him she has been watching for him through the curtains. She also tells him she had rung the hospital and that they had told her he was there. He watches as she walks ahead of him towards the scullery. He notices how much smaller she seems, as if at night she shrinks when daytime confidence flees from her body.

'Sit.' She points to the chair by the window and goes to put the kettle on. Almost immediately she returns, popping her head round the door, and looks at him for a moment before she says, 'How is she?'

'She's asleep.'

'A bad business . . . such a bad business.'

He puts his hand to his face, letting his fingers dance lightly on his cheek, and remembers the hot insistence that had burned there only an hour before.

'Are you all right, son?'

'Yeah.'

'Good man.'

She returns with a small tray and slaps it down on the tiny table, causing the large teapot to wobble. 'Sugar?'

'Yeah, two.'

'What's wrong?'

'Nothing.'

'It is two, isn't it?'

'Yeah.'

Her hands dive into the pockets of her dressing-gown and she brings out a bent cigarette, which she puts wrong way up in her mouth.

'I didn't know you smoked, Teezy.'

'I don't. Sully left me a couple.' She strikes a match and holds it precariously between the tips of her fingers, one eye squinted closed as she pulls it towards her lips.

'It's the wrong end.'

'What?'

'The cigarette. It's the wrong way round.'

'Shit.' Vigorously, she shakes the hand that is holding the lit match. It's the first time he has ever heard her curse and the word hangs in the air like a bad smell. They sit in silence for a few moments, watching the steam lift from their waiting cups of tea.

'What happened to my dad, Teezy?'

For a moment he thinks she hasn't heard him, but as he watches the small frown of concern appear above the bridge of her nose, he realises that she has.

'What do you mean?'

'You know what I mean.'

'I promised your mother.'

'Do you remember that photo you gave me when I was small?'

She nods.

'I still have it.'

Teezy returns to the kitchen. He hears the squeak of a cupboard opening and closing and the brief spurt of a tap bleeding water.

He goes to the kitchen doorway, rests against its wooden frame. She has her arms folded and is half turned away from him, He notices she is crying. He waits.

'Come and sit down.'

He follows her out of the kitchen, shadowing her all the way back to the small table, watching as she lowers her heavy body into the wooden chair, then waits for him to sit opposite her before she begins.

At around two o'clock that morning he wakes to the sound of a dog barking. It sounds like the plaintive cry of a lost soul, and it brings a shiver to James's skin. He pulls the palms of his hands across his face, and thinks of the dream that still clings to the corners of his mind. He had dreamed of the island; he had seen her shine in the black Atlantic. He had dreamed he was high on the channels of the night wind. Joy had burst across his heart, and he had felt his spirit soar, beating its way clear of his body.

He hears Teezy's snores rumbling through the house, and his dream fades like the widening ripples on a pond. Suddenly the snoring stops and the house is consumed by a still of night silence.

He remembers what Teezy had said earlier. He thinks of the two lives she had described, of the youthful patterns of their hopes and dreams, of their love and cares. He remembers how the rain had fallen outside as she told her story, falling in faint spatters against the window-pane.

PS To the Man of Light

> *Aunt Teezy's House*
> *The Centre of Newry*
> *Opposite McDowell's*
> *The Newsagents*

Dear Dad,

Let her go. Let her go. I know now, please let her go. Everyone is asleep. You could quietly just go. It is better that way. Teezy told me everything. Let us go. I know it's hard for you, and that it has been a lot for Mammy. It is over now, the secret has been shared, so let us go.

I dreamed I was with you high, high up, and that we were a part of the wind, and that she threw us this way and that. I dreamed that we were over the

237

island and that you saw the place where I was happy. It shone like a diamond in the cold night sea. I dreamed I was everywhere at once and that I was wide and free, falling through space. And I knew all the time that you were there, ready to catch me.

Don't listen to her pleas, don't come running when she calls. Be strong, as strong as the sun. Let her go. I will take care of her. No more deaths. No more wondering or fighting. Do you hear me, Dad? Do you hear me?

Love
Jimmy

28. South

The next morning Teezy brings him to the graveyard that lies on a sloping hill on the outskirts of the town. James has often seen it, from a bus or a car, its headstones glinting in the sunlight like rows of haphazard teeth. Teezy is carrying a red rose that she bought earlier in the centre of town. James had watched as she fussed over which to buy, eventually choosing one, saying, 'This one has a bit of life in it yet.'

They walk the short distance from the bus stop to the churchyard gates in silence, James slightly behind his aunt, the sun throwing long shadows on the ground ahead of them. As they reach the gate, his aunt stops, her hand resting on the heavy bolt. 'He's in here,' she says, without facing him.

She pulls the bolt back, its hard screech frightening a crow into flight. For almost the first time that morning his aunt looks at him, and nods slowly that he should enter. He brushes past her and stands on the spit gravel that covers every path leading from the gate. He stares at a grave in front of him, at its well-tended borders, and at the small posy of flowers sitting in the heart of it. It is a recent death and the air smells of upturned earth. He has never met stillness like it, a deep, final silence, as if the air has made a pact with heaven to still itself, and the world beyond seems to comply, the cars and buses on the road below moving as though through a muted haze.

They take the path leading directly down the hill, and James glances at the names cut into the passing headstones, mothers and wives, husbands and fathers, sons and daughters.

'Here he is.'

His grave is tidy, with a white granite headstone. Across the breast of the grave lies a wilting stem rose, its stalk curling back on its thorns. He watches as his aunt bends and removes it, then places her hand across his father's absent heart. 'All right, Conn?' She whispers it as if the world around her is full of listening ears. Then she places the new rose on the grave. 'I've brought little Jimmy to see you.'

Her voice is thick and hoarse. He feels angry and wants

to stop her mouth, to tell her that words have no place here, that it is a place beyond words.

She gets up and walks over to him. There is an apology in her eyes, but he is not interested: all he can see is what's left of his father – the green knobs of grass and the worn headstone, so plain and pathetic in the cold morning light.

Later that morning he phones Cathleen, braving the taunt in her father's voice, his heart banging in his chest as he hears her off-phone voice enquire who it is.

'Well, Mr Lavery.'

'Hi, Cathleen.'

'How are you?'

'All right.'

'Just all right?'

'I tried the other night.'

'I know. Is everything all right?'

'Do you want to meet?'

'I'd love to. When, James Lavery?'

'Tonight.'

'Tonight?'

'Yeah, I can get away tonight.'

'Why? Have you got something on in Dublin?'

'No.'

'It's a long way to come.'

'That doesn't matter. Do you not want to see me?'

'Of course I do. It's just . . . You're strange, James Lavery.'

'I'll ring you when I get there.'
'OK. I'll be here.'

At lunchtime he reaches his house, passing some small kids on the fringes of the estate. They hold stumps of branches in their hands, aiming them at each other, noisily ratatatting each other to death. He steps over a small, writhing body and walks up the narrow passageway at the side of his house, letting himself in through the back door. He knows Sully is there: he has seen the white van parked on the grass verge outside.

He can hear his snores, and pops his head into the living room to find him sprawled across one of the armchairs, his dirty white shirt open to the navel, his chin vibrating with every snore. His shirt is stained with runs of dried Guinness, and his hands lie at an angle off the sides of the chair, palm upwards. He looks like a drunken Christ, James thinks.

He goes upstairs and packs a small holdall, grabbing some jeans and T-shirts and stuffing them in. He takes his father's photograph from its hiding-place and, without looking at it, places it in the bag and returns downstairs.

He stands over Sully for a while, looking at the dog dribble sneaking from the side of his mouth, and the half-lidded stupor of his eyes. He sees Sully's jacket lying across the other armchair, goes through the pockets and finds his wallet. He opens it and is stunned to see a small worn photograph of him as a younger boy lying in one of its plastic windows. He looks back at Sully. Then he takes a twenty-pound note from the wallet and snaps it shut.

It is early afternoon when he reaches the hospital. His mother, he is told, has been moved to a private room as she had a bad night and disturbed the other patients. The ward sister tells him that they should have put her there in the first place, and that they were partly to blame. He nods politely, and asks if it is all right to see her. On the way to the room he is told that she already has someone with her, her friend Marion, and that she has been there for a while. The sister asks him not to be too long as visiting hours are almost over. He tells her he will only be a moment or two.

When Marion McCartan sees him she stands, walks over to him and then puts her arms round him, burying her face in his neck. He can feel the wetness of her tears. Then she lifts her head and stares at him. 'How are you, son?'

'Fine.'

'I've been sitting with her this past hour.'

He doesn't say anything. He knows she's blaming herself. He remembers their arguments and how Marion and his mother had screamed at each other all that time ago. He knows that she understands how stupid all that was now. He can see it in her eyes.

'I blame that Sully one.' She steps back from him and wipes her eyes with the tips of her fingers. 'Anyway, they say she's going to be all right, thanks be to God.' She looks at him for a moment, then says, 'I did try, son. We all tried. But she's as hard-headed . . .'

'I know you tried, Marion.' He's startled by how grown-up he sounds. He can see that what he has said has taken Marion by surprise, and for a moment she says nothing, just looks at him.

'You're a good boy, son. Maybe it'll be different now. It's got to change, James. She's got to change . . .' She goes back to the bed and looks at James's mother, running her hand across one of the bandaged wrists. 'God look after you, Annie.'

She goes, squeezing his forearm gently as she passes. For a while he just sits with her, watching her faraway sleeping face. Then he takes his father's photograph from the holdall and slips it beneath the pillow, below her sleeping head. He watches as confusion ripples across her brow, before giving way to a tiny smile. He looks at her for a moment and then around the walls of her room, his eyes scouring their plainness. Then, very softly, he leaves.

When he reaches the border he smiles to himself as he sees the familiar congregation of lorry drivers hovering around the open hatch of the mobile café, the steam rising into the air like small kidney-shaped clouds. He passes the familiar RUC Land Rover parked in its lay-by, and sees the figures of two policemen through the horizontal slats of its windows. He is sure they are making a note of him, but he continues to stare at them as he passes, with the hard eyes of a man who has nothing to lose.

He orders a coffee at the hatch, and smiles as the lady remembers him, saying, 'Hello, stranger,' in a teasing way. He takes his cup and moves across the road to sit on the same bollard, scanning the lorry drivers between sips, and watches as one walks over to talk to him. 'Long time no see.'

'Yeah . . . I've been away.'

'Young Lavery from Carrickburren, isn't that it?'

'Aye.'

'What brings you up here in the middle of the holidays?'

'I'm looking for a lift.'

'Where to?'

'Dublin.'

'Dublin no less. Is she pretty?'

James looks down at his empty cup and resents the hotness he can feel beginning in his cheeks.

'I'll be leaving for Rosslare in half an hour to catch the midnight boat to Cherbourg: I can drop you in Dublin, if you like.'

'Thanks.'

'No problem, son. Any relation of Conn Lavery is a friend of mine – and you know what they say. All roads on this island lead to Dublin. And don't let anyone tell you otherwise.'

'Half an hour?'

'Yeah, half an hour. Be there or your head's a marble.'

He watches as the man ambles back to join the other drivers. He thinks of all the deaths he has collected since he was younger, of how he has stored them like hard bright shelving amid the clutter of his thinking, and of how he now had one more to add to them. One that will cause all the others to fall away. One that will be with him until he himself dies.

'Are you right?'

He looks up to see his lorry driver waving him over.

'I forgot I have to fill her with diesel.'

He hears the roar of the engine as it growls into life, as if it is challenging the air around it. He climbs up into the cab.

'Frank O'Donnell.'

'James.'

'*Vamos.*'

James watches as Frank thrusts her into first and sees the tarmac of the border post fall away. He looks in the huge door-like mirror at its bold depiction of the world around him, and smiles as the beast of a lorry begins to carry him south.

Letter to Mammy

On the Road
Somewhere Between Newry
And Dublin
(Drogheda, I think)

Dear Mammy,

You are asleep and I'm thinking this letter as you sleep. It's a trick Dad showed me. I know you will receive it, not all of it, maybe, but some of it. I'm on my way to Dublin to see Cathleen. You haven't met her yet. I was going to tell you about her when I got home, but then . . . Well, you know . . . Don't worry about me. I'm OK . . . and you will be too when you wake up. You will be better and stronger. I left you Dad's photograph. You weren't supposed to know I had it, but now I think that's wrong. You seemed to know I had put it under your pillow because you smiled, as if everything was all right. That's why I think you will get better.

I'm sitting in a big lorry. A man called Frank

O'Donnell is giving me a lift – he says he knew Dad. I can think these things now, and I think I could even say them to you if you were here beside me.

This is what I've always wanted, to be sitting in a big lorry, moving within a big iron bear, flying past cities, and whizzing down lanes, watching all the houses go by like little boxes. But it doesn't seem important any more, not after what's happened, not after what I've been told.

Now all I want to do is stay still, to see everything slowly, in my own time, in my own way. I love you, Mammy. When you wake I want to curl up beside you and listen to you breathe.

Love, James

29. Dublin

Frank drops him at the top of O'Connell Street, and tells James to give her one for him, then winks and drives off. James watches the lorry swing back on to its route, then looks around for a phone box.

'Where are you?'

'I think I'm on O'Connell Street.'

'You mean you're not sure?'

'No.'

'What sort of an Irishman are you?'

'I don't know.'

'There's a cinema half-way down on the left-hand side as you walk towards the Liffey. Wait there and I'll come and get you.'

'OK.'

He finds the cinema and stands outside beneath its candyfloss neon, watching the faces of the people as they pass him.

'Hello, James Lavery. Eyeing up the talent?'

'No, only you.'

They walk along the banks of the Liffey, their bodies a breath's distance from each other. Eventually she stops and turns to face him. Behind her he can see the black skulk of the Liffey's surface and the dance of reflected light on its fringes from the amusement arcades across the river. She places her hands on the collar of his denim jacket and gently eases herself towards his lips. In the moment of the kiss he feels every part of him rise to meet her mouth. And for a second he feels solved.

He then thinks of his father lying in his grave. He thinks of what Teezy had told him, of the damage that the dead can do in the hearts of the living, and of the living that die in trying to reach the ones who are gone.

His hands start to tug at her clothes, tearing away at their thin layers, his fingers slipping hungrily on to the softness of her breasts. He hears her gasp in surprise, but he is oblivious to her: his hands are now in the dirt that embraces his father, ripping deep into the damp soil, pulling back the earth in a frenzy to reach him.

He feels her back arch and she tries to push him away, but he continues to maul her, grasping hard at the slats of her ribcage, at the bony husk of his father's shattered body, his fingernails blackened with the grave's secret earth.

'Stop, James! No!'

Her words reach him as though through water, as he flails in the vacuum of his father's tomb, his hand reaching deep between her legs, deep into his daddy's memory, ripping and clawing at it like a vicious cat.

'Stop! Please stop! Stop!' She wrenches herself away, and stands in front of him. 'What the hell do you think you're doing?'

He sees the anger in her eyes and hates himself.

'I thought you were different, James Lavery.'

They stand there, the air between them heavy with what has just happened, his head hanging forlornly, his hands shaking by his sides. She turns to go.

'My mother tried to kill herself last week.'

He sees her body stiffen as his words reach her. Her folded arms fall to her sides and dangle there.

'She took one of Sully's razors and ripped it across her arms.'

Slowly she turns to face him. 'Who's Sully?' she asks.

'Her . . . boyfriend. He's an arsehole.'

He doesn't realise that he has been crying until he feels her finger track the long line of moisture working its way down his face. 'Is that why . . .' she asks.

'I'm sorry.'

She holds him, reaching up to pull his body into the warmth of her embrace. 'Poor baby.'

That night he sleeps in Cathleen's father's car, a small Morris 1100. Before she goes inside to bed she sits with him for a while. 'You had me worried,' she says.

'Why?'

'I thought I'd teamed up with an animal.'

'I'm sorry.'

'Hey . . . hey . . . it's OK.'

'I don't want to go back there.'

'Won't they be worried?'

'I don't know . . . Don't care.'

'She's going to be OK, you know.'

'Yeah.'

As she leaves the car to go inside, he stops her, his hand firmly grabbing her in the crook of her arm.

'I've got to go.'

'I know . . . I know.'

'I'll come and wake you before my dad gets up for work, or there'll be hell to pay.'

'Come away with me.'

'What?'

'Come away with me for a couple of days.'

'You're cracked, James Lavery.'

'I know . . . Please.'

'No . . . Where?'

'I dunno . . . Anywhere . . . Arranmore.'

'We've just been there.'

'Let's go back, just for a couple of days.'

'No.'

'Come on! We can get a bus to Donegal Town. Let's go back.'

'Why?'

'Because . . .'

'I can't . . . I just can't.'

He watches as she sneaks back into her parents' house and smiles as she turns at the back door and blows him a kiss. He pulls up the collar of his jacket around his ears and drifts to sleep.

He is awoken by a sharp rapping noise on the car window. At first he thinks a small bird is hammering on the side of his skull, but when he opens his eyes he sees Cathleen's face beaming at him. She has a rucksack slung across her shoulder and her hair swept back off her forehead. 'Come on, then.'

'What?'

'Let's go. We've a bus to catch.'

Death by Incendiary

She watches as he plays with their child, trying hard to quell the panic she feels rising in her chest. He had told her the night before as they had lain in bed together. It was just after the moment when she had tried to coax him to make love, her hands running up and down his hard body. He had suddenly sat up, swung his legs off the bed and told her.

At first she didn't want to believe it, quietly asking God to turn the world back thirty seconds and to take her husband's words away. But his statement had hung like a fiery storm in the blackness of their bedroom.

Many times he had promised her that he was through with it, through with the violence. She hated him for it. She hated him for the leer he wore on his face whenever he spoke of Ireland as if she was a whore he could mount whenever he pleased.

She hated the so-called foot soldiers. She hated Byrne and Duffy. She hated John Farrell from the houses at the back of the estate. She hated the way they eyed her up whenever they were in the house. Above all, she hated the way they twisted Conn round their little finger, calling on him to do his duty, to fight the good fight.

She hated the searches in the middle of the night, the ignominy of clutching James to her breast, his crying ringing through the house, her husband being thrown around his own home like a distempered dog. She hated the coldness in the soldiers' eyes, the brutal high-handedness and the cold, calculated violence.

Someone had let them down. The target was a bar in

a Protestant area a few miles away. They needed someone to go in, drink a pint and leave, forgetting to take the holdall of explosives with them.

'A few less Protestants would do us all the world of good,' he had said.

'It's not funny,' she had told him.

She had told him no, she had screamed it, she had pleaded it, until she had woken little Jimmy in the next room. Teezy had arrived early that morning. She had bought James a special suit for their friend's wedding and was eager that he try it on.

Before they left, James had wanted to play with Conn in the back garden so she watches as father and son chase each other, giggling and braying with delight. It is as James starts to pretend 'kill' Conn that fury rises in her throat like a hardening fist.

She watches, trembling, as James shoots him – his body buckling like crumpled tin on to the ground – and then spears and gores his writhing body. Teezy, who has joined her at the window, asks if she's all right. She nods through her falling tears, biting hard into the back of her hand.

She strides down the garden, pulls James away from his father and yanks him towards the house. 'Come on, you've to get dressed.'

'Leave him be, Ann. We're only messing.'

'He has to get dressed and that's an end to it.'

She drinks a lot that afternoon, grabbing whatever is offered to her. At first it lifts the gloom in her and she tells herself that she is overreacting, that he has always come back from a job before, his mouth spread wide in a big, boyish grin. She has been drinking more in recent years, especially since James arrived and Conn became more and more the hard-man Republican. The gloom deepens later that afternoon when she starts on the brandys. It brings a hard frost to her eyes and an aggression to her speech.

She corners him just after the wedding cake has been cut: he is standing sipping lemonade and lime, watching the happy couple share a blissful kiss. 'I'll call the police,' she tells him.

'Piss off, Ann.'

'I promise you I'll call the police. I'll put a bloody stop to this.'

'If you call the pigs, I'll be first in the queue to do you.'

There was that look again – that hard-man Irish leer. She stands her ground, returns his hard-man stare and begins to scream. People stare, the bride and groom shoot concerned looks at her, and in the background, through a sea of heads, Teezy begins to make her way over.

She is still screaming when Conn grabs her, scoops James up in his other arm and barges his way to the garden exit. As the air hits her she stops screaming and

begins to goad him. 'You think you're fucking hard –
you all think you're so hard! Bullshit!'

'Shut up, Ann.'

'Big man Conn. Big man, little dick.'

'Shut the fuck up.'

'Make me shut up – hard man.'

She doesn't notice the small colonies of bees hovering
from flower to flower, or the gust of rose petals that
sprays into the air as they pass through the finely tended
gardens. She only sees the cold rejection in his eyes and
the attentive way he leads James to the edge of the ornate
garden pond. She watches as he whispers in their son's
ear, his hands tenderly stroking the back of the boy's
neck, and wonders where his touch for her has gone of
late.

'I've got to go,' he says, when he returns.

'Well, don't come back.'

'Don't be like this, Ann.'

'I'll be whatever way I please. It seems to suit you
fine . . . Go on, off you go, off and save the world . . .
Or destroy it – whatever fucking way you want to look
at it.'

'Fine.'

She watches as he strides back up the garden, his head
bowed, his hands thrust deep into his pockets.

'Don't go. You promised,' she whispers.

*

*The holdall exploded soon after Conn had sat down
with his pint. He was the only one killed: two others
were injured, one badly. John Farrell calls to tell her.
She hangs up half-way through his pathetic speech
about Conn being a hero and a true Irishman. The
police call round and tell her what's happened. One
smiles.*

*They won't let her see the body, or what's left of it.
There's nothing to see. He's gone and there's no bringing
him back, Teezy tells her. For hours she sits by their
window, ignoring James, who tugs at her dress. She sits
and smiles, a big fat grin. I was right, she thinks. He
wouldn't fucking listen, and I was right.*

'Shouldn't you try and rest, pet?' Teezy says.

'It'll be a closed coffin, then.'

'Yes.'

'I knew it . . . I knew it.'

30. Torn Water

As they leave Dublin they watch the fields roll by like unfurled baize, their faces turned towards the western hills. Once or twice she holds him, curling her arms round his neck and running her hands across his chest. In Donegal Town they wait for a connection to Burtonport, eating limp tomato sandwiches in a local café, then boarding the bus for the next leg of their journey. In Burtonport they stand on the familiar quay, with its webs of discarded fishing nets and odour of rotting fish. They smile as they watch the ferry-boat bounce and jostle its way between the skiffs and yachts, then come to rest against the quayside wall.

As they chug towards the island, they watch the deep, hidden water rise to cut the nose of the boat, and the clouds above them sail in a sea of sky. They see the island rise out of the ocean ahead of them, as if a giant is raising it from the depths only for their eyes.

He thinks of the quayside they have just left, of how small and frightened Sully had seemed when he had stood there with Manus only a week before. He sees his mother's body held by the man of light. He sees Teezy's sorrow as she had told him his parents' story, which had held them together in silence all these years.

They wave impulsively at the fishermen who sit on Arranmore quay, their match-thin roll-ups in their mouths, eyes fixed far out to sea. As they step on to the concrete of the dock Cathleen pulls on his arm, jolting him into a run, pulling him up the road past the café and out towards the far side of the island.

At the top of the first hill they slow as the wide lift of the horizon comes into view, and stop to watch. James imagines them flying through the thin seam where the sky meets the sea, for ever held in the misty world of birds and building rain.

They run down the hill, their rapping feet beating out their enthusiasm for one another, their heads lifted high by the sudden gusts of wind. The sun is lowering as they reach the headland, throwing soft, crimson light on to the underbellies of the clouds. They slip quietly down on to the beach, their feet welcoming its soft give.

They find a rock pool and sit by it, watching the

foraging of small crabs and the lilting sway of seaweed: fascinated by the completeness of its world, by the sealed fervour of its life, from the pinhead shrimp to the pincer-waving posturing of the larger crabs. James watches as they break from a nook of rock and scuttle to the middle of the pool, stirring up small plumes of sand, then threaten the vast mystery of the world above with their lofted claws and disappear once more. He looks at the flies on the surface of the pool, their long legs drawing elegant patterns on the water.

Cathleen has pulled away from him and run to the far end of the beach. He sees her bending down to pull at some driftwood before returning with a long shank. He stands and watches as she draws their names in the sand, in big, bold strokes. He turns back to the rock pool, and looks once more at the water. Suddenly the wind drops and the pool clears, the long tramlines of ripples giving way to a placid shine.

He is being carried. Through high imposing rooms, the hands that are around him are big and calloused, but delicate in the way they hold him. He sees the ornate ceilings above him pass by as they go through room after room. At the beginning of the garden he is put down. One of the large hands enfolds his and he feels safe, held in the territory of his father's heart. He looks up and his father gives him one of his strong, secret smiles. They enter the garden of the hotel, blinking as the sunlight floods their eyes. The boy points excitedly at the bees that hover in the air like tiny striped Zeppelins, and at the sudden flurry of rose petals that litter the air.

They reach the small pond at the bottom of the garden and peer into its dark depths. He can remember his father's reflection towering into view, filling the hushed calm of the pond, his face held in its secret world. 'Wait here for me, Jimmy.'

He remembers the cruel arguments that had filled the air that morning, like the sound of knives being sharpened. He remembers his mother's hard features and the savage blur of her fists on his father's chest.

'Wait here, Jimmy, I won't be long.'

He feels his father's hands leave his shoulders, giving them a small squeeze of comfort before they go. He remembers watching his father's reflection disappear from the face of the pond as if the sky had suddenly claimed him.

Early that morning they had played their game, in the small garden at the back of their house. He remembers the feel of the stripped tree branch in his small hands, he remembers his father telling him to close his eyes, and hearing his big feet crashing among the rosebushes as he sought a hiding-place.

'Make a machine-gun . . . Jimmy, make a machine-gun.'

He remembers lifting the branch up to the cross-hairs of his eyes and scouring the undergrowth for his father.

262

Suddenly his father had broken from the cover of his rosebush, scattering soft pink petals high into the air.

'Don't shoot! Don't shoot!'

'Ratatat, ratatat, ratatat!'

'No, please! Please don't shoot!'

'Ratatat, ratatat, ratatat.'

His father had staggered towards him, legs shuddering, face contorted with pain. He can remember giggling.

'You got me, Jimmy – you got me good.'

He had watched as his father rolled on the grass, legs kicking in the air. He remembers turning the machine-gun into a knife, a spear, a bow. He 'killed' his father in many different ways that morning, squealing with pleasure as his daddy rolled and writhed on the patchy grass of the garden.

Teezy had told him that she and his mother had watched them from the kitchen window until his mother could stand it no more. She had marched down the garden to pluck him from the game and yank him into the house.

And later that day, as he stood where he had been put by his father, gazing into the muddy pond, he could hear his parents arguing behind him, their voices lowered in case he heard them. Teezy had told him they were at a wedding, a friend of his mother's was getting married, but at some point his father had needed to slip off as he had a prior engagement. It was this that he and his mother had been rowing about.

Now, all those years later, as he stands gazing into the rock pool he can remember how fiercely he had concentrated his gaze on the surface of that pond, his face a tight ball of focus, his small fists clenched as he fought to ignore the row taking place behind him. All this he had buried, stored deep within his heart, until Teezy's story the other night had wakened it from its uneasy slumber. Now as he stands by water, separated by time and distance, he sees that small boy fighting the ripples that are obscuring his world. He sees also the small beat of light that leaves his chest, rising into the air like the flash of a mirror in sunlight, or the moving negative of a bird in flight. He watches as it folds itself into the pond, burrowing deep into its sediment.

He remembers the feeling of loss as he watched his light disappear into the cool water, as if all colour was bleeding from the world. He hears his mother's voice, her pleas, her threats, her insults as she battles with his father.

'Don't go,' she had said. 'You promised.'

He feels Cathleen's arms coil round his shoulders, her hands playing lightly on his chest, her lips on the back of his neck. 'Come on . . . I've something to show you.'

He looks at her, at the strong high colour of her face, the pink of her cheeks, and he smiles. He sees the curl of the clouds behind her head, and the pencil-line hills